Out of Date

Out of Date

Helen Walker

Copyright ©2024 Helen Walker

The moral right of the author of this work has been asserted in accordance with the Copyright, Designs and Patents Act 1988.

This book is a work of fiction. Names, character, places and incidents are either the product of the author's imagination or are used fictitiously. Any resemblance to actual people living or dead, events or locales is entirely coincidental.

All rights reserved. No part of this book may be reproduced, transmitted or stored in an information retrieval system in any form or by any means, electronic, graphic or mechanical, including photocopying, recording or taping without prior permission in writing from the copyright owner

ISBN: 9798336112849

A CIP catalogue record for this book is available from the British Library

Visit Helen Walker online at www.helenwalkerauthor.com

For Mel

Who was all things love, laughter and friendship.

Sleep well beautiful

Prologue

After many terrible choices, dreadful dates and a small number of divorces, some might say that I should've given up on any idea of love and romance. That I should just accept the fact that I was going to be a honky old woman surrounded by 15 dogs, 2 cats and a pooping parrot.

I didn't want that to be my future. Why should it be? Why should anyone just accept that? I didn't want to give up and be the old woman who had served her purpose and had her chance. I wanted to actually *connect* with a real someone and not in a desperate 'anyone is better than no one' kind of way either.

Some people are simply in love with the *idea* of being in love. They adore those first few months where everything is shiny and new. Each one of you on your best behaviour. Still in that stage where you pretend that farting, leg shaving, and all things bathroom-related don't happen. The new and shiny can't last because life isn't a Disney movie.

The people who can only pretend to be something they're not, well, they aren't keepers. When things become real, and they *will* become real, the pretenders move on like a magpie. They move onto the next shiny object of their affections.

I'd had more than my fair share of the 'love to be in love but can't handle real life' kind of guy, and I refused to order from that menu again.

They say there's someone for everyone, and I'd kissed enough frogs, and believed enough bloody lies trying to find mine. Yet the sod eluded me.

Surely it wasn't impossible. I needed to believe that I still had a chance of finding that one person after relationship disasters and divorce. I mean, Jennifer Aniston managed it, so why couldn't I?

Hell, I wasn't some empty market stall at the end of a busy Saturday that only had the squashed tomatoes and bruised fruit left on offer.

Damn it! I still had a lot to offer. I had a good career, my own house and bloody good teeth.

I'd raised my kids to a more independent age and paid my dues in more ways than I cared to count. There had to be more to life than single-person hobbies, and the lure of a pension plan that wouldn't buy a single bog roll by the time I got there.

I looked in the mirror, really looked. I wasn't bad. Yes, time had changed more than my face, but everything was still [mostly] where it was supposed to be without surgery or ugly shapewear. When I smiled, I quite liked the little lines around my eyes, they were part of my journey. My journey had given me strength…. and grey hairs… hair dye took care of those little buggers though. I wasn't ready to accept a badger stripe just yet.

I could have done without the sparse eyelashes too; they were a total let down. Thank you, mother.

For someone who had already lived half of their life [and made a spectacular balls-up of most of it] surely the second half would be a vast improvement.

I decided, there and then. I was ready. It was time to get back out there. It was time to raise hope with a glass of wine and a decent bra and get back out there.

Out where though?

I looked at the statistics. Single mum, 3 kids, 2 dogs, 3 divorces and the final number, 53. My age, fifty bloody three.

So, to the big question…. was there anyone out there who wasn't an arsehole? Someone who was a genuinely awesome person… someone who didn't have the personality of Frank Gallagher and the looks of Mr. Burns?

The other big question of course…. could that someone look past the stunning statistics of my life and actually *see* me? I'd had enough of feeling invisible.

And if there was someone out there, how the hell would I find them?

Because the one thing that I knew…. they weren't going to find me. I basically didn't go anywhere. Other than the odd night out with friends, my life was kids, work, kids, home, sleep…. Everyday. Rinse and bloody repeat.

My many job titles include referee to bickering kids, trainer to anti-social dogs, oh, and line manager to a work team so young that I could have birthed their parents.

There were times that I thought I must have been Attila the Hun in a past life, because my love-life in *this* one felt like it had been my payback. But in the spirit of positivity, I was sure that the universe was overdue to be kind to me. Either that, or she really was a bitch who deserved the curses I threw at her daily.

With my decision made, there was one rather chuffing huge problem…. where did I start?

I needed to call upon the help of the only people I trusted with this.

I needed the help of the cluster of cackling wonders who'd held my hand through all the laughter, tears and snot.

I needed my friends.

Date 1

My brilliant friends [or the coven as I preferred to call them] had promised me that one day, I would be ready, and that they'd be there when I was.

They are, apart from one singleton, all happily married to great people and I'm lucky to have them in my life. They'd seen me through the highs, lows and lowers of the past 35 years.

The coven was happy to hear that, at last, I was ready to step back into the sun.

'About bloody time!' was their collective response.

After 3 single years of disgusting honesty about the reasons behind my lifelong terrible man-choices, for which I partly blamed my absentee arsewipe of a father, I felt ready to ask my friends to help me to find a date.

They used words like 'funny, intelligent, articulate and an all-round brilliant person' to describe me. Those words make an amazing CV for a job in the caring profession, but that didn't mean a guy would notice those qualities.

In my experience, blokes tended to notice, shall we say, physical attributes first. A bit like looking at pizza, getting drawn in by the topping and not noticing whether it was deep-pan or thin base. Some people just wanted a conversation with your boobs, and your personality was an afterthought.

My friends assured me that, just like a football delivered by DPD, I was an 'all-round package'.

"So, do you know anyone who might fancy an all-round package?' I looked at them hopefully.

I'd figured that as my previous choices were a cracking set of narcistic liars, wankers and can't keep it zipped cheaters, my friends would know the way forward.

I really thought that they'd jump at the chance to undertake a mission for their bestie and find me someone deliciously decent that I could connect with. Surely, they knew of someone….

My request was met with tumbleweed, not a little tumbleweed, but a fucking mountainous tumbleweed, whipping across the Gobi Desert.

'Erm, most people I know are already in relationships.'

'Yeah,' the others agreed, 'or married.'

With my decision made, I wasn't accepting their feeble excuses. They must know *someone*. I assured them that they could do this, hell, I practically begged them. I'd prepared a list of simple requirements.

Such a simple list that I'd written them down.

Type of person
- Personality [a nice one please] A person needs a personality.

- A sense of humour was a must. Life needed laughter, my life needed laughter.
- Honest [as much as any human can be]
- And they must have a soul. Have you any idea how many soulless knobheads there are in this world? Lots.

It also goes without saying that in relationships, there must be a mutual physical attraction, a person can only fake that for so long. You need to look at your partner and think 'Phwoar', unless they're picking their nose or something equally gross of course, but generally you need the phwoar.

No matter what your personal take on attractive is, when you first meet someone, there must be that moment where you really want to get down to some intimate business. Obviously, hands off until permission is given or there will be an arrest, but at the *very least*, you need to be thinking about it from the start.

As a result, I'd been brutally honest about the physical attributes that I wanted/needed.

Physical things
- Hair, own hair of course, no toupees.
- Own teeth
- Preferably tall, definitely taller than me
- No pregnant beer bellies

- Broad shoulders but not overly muscle bound, I didn't want to have to fit in dates around his gym schedule

One married friend finally stepped forward with her offering.

The lovely Rachel leaned forward, 'Well, there is a guy at work….'

After grabbing my attention with statements like 'he's funny, lovely, caring', etc, etc, she then happily presented me with a photo of him and waited expectantly.

He was approximately 5 feet tall and had a head that resembled a swimming cap…. with tufts. That pool accessory noggin glared and gleamed from her phone screen. The song from Moana immediately sprang to mind….. 'Shiny'.

Did she even read my list? After 30 years of adoring this friend, I began to wonder if she even liked me.

I protested loudly, 'Bugger off! He's probably very lovely, but he'd come up to my left nipple and…what is with that ear fringe? Nope!'

So, with little to no choice, and on the advice of Charlotte, whom I considered to be my non-related sister, I embarked upon the terrible and horrifying world of online dating.

Charlotte had recently joined an online dating site, 'It's fun! Yeah, there are some dickheads, but you can sift those out and concentrate on the decent ones,' she assured me.

'Ok, so how do I do it?'

The idea, apparently, is that you concoct a profile consisting mostly of lies and select an age you'd still like to be. Next, you upload photos of yourself, no distractions of attractive friends on them [so my friends were not allowed to be in the pics, beautiful bitches that they were]

The photos needed to be about 10 years out of date. The more cleavage exposed, either butt or boob, the better. Then, you declare that you're 'up for anything'.

Well, I'm not 'up for anything', so being an honest[ish] person, I did none of that. I decided on a real and quite honest profile.

Profile Info
- Freya, 53
- Researcher and general dogsbody in a public service [no company name]
- Green eyes [occasionally bloodshot]
- Long brown hair [assisted by hair dye when I remember]
- Normal/Athletic[ish] build
- Religion [as and when required]

I added a photo taken that very day - the 6th one to be exact, on two of them they'd caught me speaking so I looked like a wide-mouthed frog.

I added a firm declaration of 'Nope, not up for anything, I have some standards.'

Next came the list of likes and dislikes. My fingers hovered; I wondered what I was supposed to put.

If I was going to be super honest, it would have read like a cross between a nerd and a knobhead had written it. It wouldn't hurt to embellish this part, would it? I mean, I didn't want it to be a complete lie because I'm not a fan of liars, but a *tidgy* bit of tweaking on the truth here would be okay.

Together, the coven decided that, amongst other things,

I liked
- Literature [True]
- History [True again]
- Beach holidays [Lie. I hate sand and I melt quicker than a Mr Whippy ice-cream in the sun]
- Lazy Sunday mornings [Lie, well, maybe. It had been over 15 years since I'd even had the chance to check. Selfish kids]

I disliked
- Cheap wine [a half-lie, I'd drink it but would probably moan about it]
- Brown shoes [Totally true. Brown clothing and footwear should be outlawed for all of eternity]
- Avocados [What? Random and a lie. They might look like dragon bogeys but they're actually quite tasty]

And then, I clicked create.

Suddenly, there I was. A real person, a genuine age, an honest as possible profile and requirements of who and what I was looking for [own hair and teeth mentioned first, of course]

I'd also added that I was that statistical marvel.....a single parent. My kids were a huge part of my life, they took time and were the priority. I couldn't, and wouldn't, hide the fact that I'd got them.

Too right. The coven all agreed. Anyone who hid the fact that they had kids were either a shit parent, or they were only in it to get laid. I hoped I was neither.

I wasn't expecting much in the way of any responses. My friends were far more hopeful, or perhaps, more pissed than I was.

I wondered if my lack of expectation came from the old saying 'don't expect much and you can only be pleasantly surprised' but my lack of expectation was certainly met in those first few hours.

Almost immediately, I got several responses. I got the predators.

Brad, 37. Profile pic of Brad in a gimp mask. His tag line was short 'requires dominant woman.'

His message was also brief, *"Hey, you looking for me?"*

Erm, No Brad, No I'm not.

Geoff, 40 [yeah, maybe 20 years ago Geoff] Professional, divorced, looking for 'fun times, no strings and stiletto heels.'

It's no wonder you're divorced Geoff, you look better in heels than most women I know.

His message was equally stunning, *"Hey beautiful, what size shoe are you?"*

Not your size Geoff.

Alex, 57. Gym bunny posing with what looked like plasticine muscles.

Alex had offered to share his 'special protein shake' with me.

A kind offer Alex, I'm sure, but no. Thank you.

The coven zoomed in on his photo, it looked like someone had shoved 3 peas down his speedos.

Dave, 46. Love me, love my 2 chins and 3 teeth.

Dave had obviously put a great deal of thought into his message, *"Hi."*

That was his effort.

Mine was to delete his lengthy missive.

Marcus, 51. Selfie taken in a mirror in his bedroom. In his eagerness to take his photo, Marcus had omitted to check his surroundings.

Filthy bedsheets and a box of tissues on the bedside cabinet.

His message was equally as gross, *"Hey, wanna bang?"*

No Marcus. The only thing I'd 'wanna bang' into you is a left hook to your surprisingly small jaw.

***

Let's face it, it wasn't a great start. These guys must get notifications when some poor sacrificial lamb wanders into the field. Like wolves, they pounce trying to get their teeth into that newby flesh with their outstanding messages.

After lamenting the lack of anything genuinely interesting, my friends decided to search through the profiles on offer. I watched over my glass of wine as my phone was passed around by their eager hands, and I wondered if it would just be better to delete the profile and accept my fate as Yorkshire's elderly Bridget Jones.

As it turned out, their poking and prodding of profiles led to date number 1.

'Oooh, what about this one? He seems nice!' my married friend, Sarah, poked the screen under my nose.

Jason, 48, seemingly own hair and teeth. Ex-military [no indication of what he was actually doing now] He lived 20 miles away.

No kids. Financially stable… I'd been warned by my non-related sister that most people lie about that. No one is going to put skint, up to the eyeballs in debt, so it must be taken with a pinch of salt.

Jason declared that he had sense of humour, this was yet to be established of course. Many people find themselves hilarious, whilst those around them die of boredom.

However, he liked the same books and films, and he went hiking… so maybe outdoorsy, unless he meant walking round to the local off-licence.

After much cajoling by the coven, and against my better judgement, I agreed to meet him for coffee during the day, in a public place. My friends were going to be planted in the café, en masse, in case of a kidnapping attempt.

I was surprised at how nervous I felt. Normally, I'm someone who goes into meetings without the nervous jitters and dry gob, but this was very different. It felt like a personal judgement.

Mainly because it was.

He would be judging me as much as I would be judging him. He might have a list of criteria that he'd created with his friends…. *"No dragons, no moustaches and definitely, no 6th toes."* I checked myself over, I thought I'd pass. I didn't turn into a raging wyvern at midnight, had no 'tash and only had 5 [rather oddly] shaped toes on each foot.

Good to go.

As I've always had a major dislike of being late for anything, I'd set off a bit early to get parked up. As I was scrabbling in my purse for some parking change, my phone pinged .I half hoped he'd cancelled, so I could avoid the whole awkward scene and just have a coffee with my friends. I only checked the message as I was about to walk into the cafe.

And what a shocker…. he hadn't cancelled. Instead he'd sent me a photo of him in his military dress coat….. in a fucking mop cupboard.

The fact that he'd got no trousers on escaped me at first, the mops distracted me. I'm not sure what I was more horrified at, the fact that he'd thought I'd be impressed by his red jacket and Y-Fronts combo, or that he was in a mop cupboard.

I forwarded the photo to the covens' chat and said, *"No feckin way."*

My text was met with *"But you're here, we can see you and so will he. Give him a chance. You can do this!"*

Against my better judgement, which as previously established, was poor at best in these situations, I went inside to meet mop cupboard man.

And that's the awkward bit, you can't walk in somewhere for a date looking like a hawk scanning for its prey, you need to look casual and relaxed. I headed straight for the counter, ordered my coffee and clocked my friends sat in the back doing the eye wiggle to a figure sat in the corner. Mop guy.

Trying to not to highlight that I'd slopped scalding hot coffee over my thumb, I approached him. My heart had already sunk upon receipt of that bloody photo, and now, it sank even further. 20lbs heavier and half a head of hair less sat waiting for me.

'Hi, Jason is it?' Of course it was, there was no mistaking him.

'The very same. Raya, yeah?' he stared at my chest as he got my name wrong, 'Did you get me a coffee?'

What? Have I fuck… I tried to smile, 'Oh, erm, sorry, I thought you'd have got one already.'

I wasn't about to offer to waste any more money on this date.

'No worries, I can maybe share yours, eh? Joking.'

Funny. Knobhead.

As I reluctantly sat down, he went to get himself a coffee. I noticed his sandalled feet; he hadn't even bothered to clean *or* trim his toenails. Yellow talons fought for freedom from the end of his dirty sausage toes… and I fought the urge to vomit.

The conversation that followed was one-sided. His sided. If I was being gracious, I would say that it was because he was nervous, but I'm not that gracious. The guy just loved talking about himself. The only time he stopped was to slurp and gulp his coffee.

Two [of many] things that are an issue for me, I dislike one sided conversation, and I completely bloody loathe noisy eaters, guzzlers and gulpers.

Jason also happily told me that I was the first of 4 dates that he'd lined up for that day. He had high hopes for date number 3 though because she was petite and blonde with big boobs, but I was a 'decent start'.

Generous of you Jason.

He then asked what I'd thought of his dress jacket photo because, apparently, women 'go mad for it'.

What was I supposed to say? You look like a pervy janitor, who nicked a jacket from his mum's dressing-up box and forgot the trousers.

All I could manage was. 'Well, it was different.'

'Yeah babe, they broke the mould when they made me,' he emphasised with a Fonzie finger point.

It wasn't just his feet that were cheesy.

I resisted the urge to say, 'they didn't just break the mould, they smashed the shit out of it so they couldn't repeat their terrible mistake.'

The final straw was his evident love of collecting, or rather, creating roadkill. His glee at hitting helpless creatures with his Volkswagen Polo screamed serial killer. I couldn't sit there a moment longer. I feigned stomach cramps and told Jason that I could feel a nasty bout of diarrhoea coming on, it might be contagious, and I needed to leave. Now.

Quite frankly, I would rather walk butt-naked through Leeds train station on match day, than to have to sit there a moment longer listening to his murderous monologue.

My friends soon caught up with me laughing as they asked, 'Well?'

'I'd rather eat my own vomit. I nearly did. He's fucking disgusting.'

'So, not what you were looking for then?' they laughed, 'There are plenty more…'

I cut them off, 'Don't say fish in the sea. I'm attracting the bottom dwellers, the loaches and the stinking suckermouth catfish. Where's Aquaman when you need him?'

I doubted Marvel or DC would ever fight over making the film *'Mop Man, The Long Road to Kill.'*

I reached for my phone and did the only decent thing I could for my safety and sanity, I blocked him.

It was NOT a great start to what was supposed to be an exciting adventure. In fact, it could be said that it was a totally shit start.

Surely, it could only get better….

Date 2

The next few days were filled with domestic drudgery, work wonders and of course, many *unsuitable "Hiya luv, you look fit,"* kind of messages from the inarticulate gene pool.

Oh, and then there was a message from Jack who decided to tell me that he was rubbing his dick whilst looking at my profile pic.

Too much information Jack. Too. Much. Fucking. Information.

Disillusioned with the whole online dating crud and concerned that Mop Man would suddenly appear on my doorstep with a pair of squished rabbits, I concentrated on pairing socks from the odd sock bag.

It's the place where lonely socks go to live out their single lives, without much hope of ever finding their partner in foot covering happiness.

Then it dawned on me. I was just some old odd sock. Faded from the washing machine of life with little hope of finding my foot covering 'sole' mate.

'How bloody depressing.' I sighed and carried on with

the search in the crumpled Tesco's carrier bag. My phone pinged. Dating site message. It couldn't be the serial killer; I'd blocked him. Curiosity got the better of me and I read it.

"Hiya, how's it going? Hope you're managing to traverse the weirdo's and hobbits on here."

Hmm, okay. He's nicely used the word 'traverse' and hadn't [so far] mentioned massaging his dick, so, I read his profile.

Paul, 49. Landscape gardener.

Fairly local, liked art, poetry and history. Decent height, one chin. Hair and teeth present and woah! He'd quoted Andrew Marvell, 17th century satirical poet and curly haired wonder. *"Lady, you deserve this kind of dedication – and I don't want to accept any lesser kind of love."*

Blimey! A bit bloody obscure but the English graduate in me was [easily] impressed… and totally ignored the fact that Marvell's poem went on to say that worms would take the lady's virginity when she died.

My lamenting of life in the sock bag was momentarily forgotten. I decided to message him back.

I stood there in my dog slobbered pyjamas and oversized dressing gown, looking like the pigeon lady from Home Alone 2. I needed to respond with something witty, nothing flirty though, far too early for that. Witty was what I needed.

Ten minutes and much overthinking later, I responded, *"Traversing quicker than a gladiator on Hang Tough."*

Then, for some unknown reason, I added *"The purpose of our lives is to be happy.... Or end up online dating"* ...**Quote:** *half Dalai Lama, half me.*

Yep, witty and educated, that's me.

Paul didn't reply.

Well, bollocks to you Paul.

Bollocks to YOU, and that particular quote, mate, is all mine.

I felt a bit of a tit after that. Like a kid learning guitar, I couldn't seem to strike the right chord with anyone and was starting to feel a bit out of my depth. I reported back to the coven on the state of my non-dates. Their overwhelming verdict was that maybe what *I thought* I wanted, just wasn't that realistic.

'Maybe ease up on your list and look for something different, something *off-list*,' Charlotte suggested.

'Yeah, compromise on it a bit. It can't hurt,' Sarah agreed.

What? No and NO! The outcome of 3 years self-reflection was that I'd compromised myself for most of my adult love-life. Bloody compromise is why I'd stayed in relationships, knowing they were hurtling at the speed of light towards the morgue of marriage. I wasn't going to do that again. It was just not worth the heartache for anyone.

I sulked and ran myself a bath. Laying in the bath is not really the place to check your online dating messages, there's an overwhelming sense of vulnerability and well, nakedness.

I was also suitably paranoid that my man thumbs would unwittingly press camera mode and post a photo back. Sending an image of something that's risen from hell's bog, rather than a glamourous mermaid, was not a comforting thought. So, I ignored the pings until I was safely dressed.

James, 51. Civil servant.

There seemed to be a lot of people lurking under that particular umbrella title.

James was divorced, had kids and yes! He was 6 foot 4. So far, so good. Even considering that most people put inches on their profile, he had to at least be tall-ish. He'd also been to see similar bands and was arty.

He liked eating in. He liked eating out [a common profile filler] and he'd offered a simple, non-offensive message, *"Hey, how's your day been?"*

I'm not going to tell you how my day has really been, James. Moaning about regurgitated pizza on the step into work, wiping wee off the toilet seat [again] or the argument with the tosser in the BMW who tried to kill me, were not hot topics. So, I lied. *"Good so far, you?"*

Back and forth. It turned out that James was actually quite funny.

He seemed genuinely interested in me [huzzah] and he didn't mention his dick once. Bonus.

So, we arranged coffee. Different café this time, I didn't want them thinking I was picking up randomers to fill the void in my lonely life [as if]

Safety friend arranged. The outfit was carefully selected. My hair had been given some much-needed attention and I looked half decent for once. With a packet of Polo's stashed in the pocket [coffee breath is not attractive] I arrived a few minutes early.

James wasn't hard to spot, he was indeed wonderfully tall. Maybe not 6' 4, but tall, none the less *and* he got up when I went over to his table. Awesome start. As I sat down, I clocked Sarah nodding her approval and doing a sly thumbs up.

That was the high point. James, it turned out, had a lot to say about his ex-wife.

Fifteen minutes in and the bitterness was palpable. I knew all about her cheating. How she'd taken him to the cleaners, financially, not literally. James had dodgy stains on his jeans…. in rather odd places.

He told me all about how she got the car. It seemed that James was more attached to the car than he was to his own kids. By that point I was giving my friend the 'Please save me' signal, and my facial expressions had frozen into the botox non-smile I'd seen on Love Island clips.

I needed to leave before I gave James a swift kick in the shin and a subscription to Car Lovers Monthly. My friend, sensing my Jedi 'get me the hell out of here' mind trick, came over panting like she'd been chasing Usain Bolt.

'I'm so glad… I found you, there's been …a break-in at work, we…. need you to do the…. insurance thingy. Now!'

I thought she was going to hyperventilate.

She'd done so well on the fake running pant; she just lost it a bit at the end. Still, it did the trick. I excused myself, wished James all the best in the recovery of his car, and left. Never to cross comms again.

***

I drove home wondering what the hype over online dating was all about. Dating was bad enough when you'd arranged it in person, but at least you'd already seen them. You'd spoken to them face to face and made the decision that they were worth your time and the £2.50 price of a coffee. Online dating was just soul destroying.

I wondered how people found someone online that they want to tangle their lives with, when I couldn't even find someone that I wanted to have a second coffee with.

Somewhat deflated, I got home and cursed the pile of ever-present chores staring me in the face. Then I remembered, it was bloody parents evening.

Gah! Ten minutes with each teacher. Crammed into a sweaty hall, over-filled with clashing perfumes from the other single mums who were all trying to get extra minutes with poor Mr Wilson. The thought did nothing to lighten my mood.

Parents evening was one of those rare occasions that gave parents a fleeting sense of power. In the few days leading up to it, we could threaten to tell the teachers just *who* had finished that last project build, and the kids believed it. In those precious few days, the children were almost pleasant, and a parent felt majestic.

Rocking up to high school parents evening was very different to primary school. At primary school we had ten minutes with one teacher, who covered every subject.

We were in, out and [usually] praised the offspring on the way home. Even better was the new option to chat over the phone. If the teacher couldn't be arsed to conduct a face-to-face appointment, it meant you didn't have to hunt through the wardrobe to find clean clothes. Job done.

High school presented a new challenge. There was a teacher to speak to for each subject that our little wonders took, and I had two of them in high school, so it took twice as long.

As I was getting older, the teachers were getting younger, and their eyebrows were getting bigger.

Sitting there mesmerised by Miss Religious Studies' two slugs battling for dominance on her face, I paid no attention to how my son was performing in that class.

Next, it was Mrs History lesson. Her verbatim

reading of my daughter's report, which I'd already received, did nothing to impress me. Unlike her rogue brow. She hadn't slicked one eyebrow down quite as well as the other. The left brow was reaching for freedom, and I walked away feeling sorry for it.

Eventually, my time came to see poor old Mr Wilson, the art and design teacher. I say poor and old, but the guy was young and surprisingly good looking. He always seemed genuinely embarrassed by the attention his looks brought him.

The line of mums trying to catch his eye was probably one of the oddest things to happen in that assembly hall. Although, Year 8's Roblox rendition of Mid-Summer Night's Dream came in a close second.

The army of pushed up boobs heading toward Mr Wilson's frightened face, was alarming.

I elbowed my way through. *Piss off Penelope, I've got a pizza waiting for me at home, and I'm fucking hungry.*

Poor Mr Wilson seemed relieved that I was obviously too old for the boob thrust. I hadn't even bothered brushing my hair for the appointment with him. He finally seemed to breathe. Poor man.

With polite thank you's exchanged, I gathered up my gangly humans, told them they were completely awesome, and headed home.

The pizza had waited far too long for my attention.

Date 3

With all memories of women squeezed into sausage-skin dresses forgotten, I got on with the evening. Once the offspring, who had nicked most of the pizza, retired into their festering rooms, I decided to have one last snoop around the profiles on offer.

Nothing new.

Brad in his mask, still hoping to find his gimpy soulmate and Paul, no doubt ignoring any response he got [it surely couldn't be that my overthought response was the cause of the snub]

Then appeared **Toby, 49.**

Decent profile giving lots of hooks, interesting indeed. Tall and again, not too far away. In his profile pic, he had such a lovely smile and a full head of hair.

Hello Toby! Did I dare send him a message? I'd kind of sat back so far and waited for someone to message me but as the coven had said, I needed to be pro-active. But what would I say?

It's so much easier to respond [or not] to someone else's icebreaker than it is to plunge the ice pick in and do the job yourself. I found myself talking out loud, 'Hi Toby', 'Hey you'.

Oh, for god's sake. I realised that I was being pathetic, and it annoyed me. A lot. So, I sent a simple hello and an image of a pea pod in reference to his favourite film. I had to Google it.... I'd never watched Invasion of the Body Snatchers; The Lion King was far more me.

But I was, after all, attempting to show him that I had actually bothered to read his profile. And, rather chuffed with myself, I pressed send.

Toby didn't reply straightaway, that was ok, I'm not some desperate saddo sat there expecting a reply within nanoseconds, but after 20 minutes I got bored of waiting and went and scoffed some toast.

On the last mouthful, Toby replied. He even apologised for the delayed response. Very polite Toby, well done sir.

Several hundred messages later, we thought it would be good to meet up. I checked that a safety friend was free.

"Got another date!! Anyone free to chaperone? This guy seems nice." Grinning emoji.

Rachel replied, *"Ooooh, Me! Exciting. See you there!"*. Party hat emoji.

And just like that, it was arranged.

I felt rather smug. I'd instigated that and now felt quite triumphant. I'd finally gained some control over my online dating destiny. Or so I thought.

***

The day of the date arrived and instead of feeling nervous, I was looking forward to this coffee date. I looked at myself, 'Hmm, not bad.'

I'd chosen a nice top and jeans that held everything in place. For the first time in a long time, I felt good.

After a last check of the teeth for any signs of breakfast, I went in with a big grin. There he was, true to his profile pic and as tall as he had claimed to be, huzzah!

The conversation was really easy, and the laughter seemed genuine. I was beginning to think that Toby could well be a second coffee. Until he dropped a couple of bombs, and I don't mean that he farted.

Bombshell #1

I had noticed in his profile blurb, that Toby hadn't mentioned his job. There was a reason for that. Toby was an undertaker, and not the wrestling kind.

"I've been an undertaker for over 20 years. It's not something I tend to advertise. People either take the piss or run a mile" he explained.

Oh dear.

"Wow, that's… interesting. You'll always have work though, eh." That was all I could manage.

Yes, it's an incredibly honourable job and something that takes a very special kind of person to be able to do. But try as I might, I just couldn't help but wonder where Toby's hands had been. I kept looking at them as he talked, wondering when they'd last held the cold, lifeless limb of Great Uncle Bulgaria. I could only hope that he'd washed his hands, vigorously.

It's no wonder he'd left it off his profile. It would take a very special kind of lady to be able to look at those hands and not feel a bit icky, and I just wasn't that special.

Bombshell # 2

Toby really didn't like kids. I mean, he was very venomous in his dislike of children. Of any age. I wasn't looking for a replacement dad for my kids, they had one of those. Yes, he was an arsehole that constantly cancelled on them, but he was still their father.

I was genuinely shocked. Had Toby not read my bloody profile? It clearly stated that I have [not so] small humans. I had to point that out to Toby.

'Oh. Right. I don't really read people's profiles. Well, you haven't *always* got them, have you?' He looked hopeful.

Erm, yes Toby. They're my children, not indigestion, you dickhead.

So, Toby and I parted ways [without touching hands] I did wish him best of things. I just couldn't imagine those cold slabby hands on me, whilst I waved the kids off to Timbuktu. Forever.

***

Friday night came around and the coven gathered in a bar. My non-related sister was having a great time dating various profile owners and was happily [and openly] dating three guys at once.

"Dating, *not* shagging,' she was quick to point out.

I just didn't know how she found the energy. I could only look on in admiration [and slight envy] at her evident joy of dating life.

After sharing my experience of Toby, the non-wrestling, kid hating, undertaker. I told them about the 18 dick pics, in various states of attention, that I'd kindly received, and declared that, perhaps, online dating was not for me after all.

Once they'd stopped laughing, the overwhelming decision of the coven was that, if I wanted to take this seriously, I was on the wrong dating site.

I went to the bar for much needed refills and when I got back, discovered that I'd been signed up for a so called 'professionals' site. Who knew there was such a thing?

'There, all done!' Sarah showed me, 'Take a look.'

A new profile pic had been selected, I was half smiling in this one, and apparently, I was all good to go. They'd even paid the subscription. Thank you, ladies!

The conversation turned to everything but blokes on dating sites. Looking round the pub it seemed like everyone was in a couple, togetherness was everywhere.

Some people find themselves feeling left out and depressed about that, but as I watched the arguments brewing as the beer flowed, I was kind of glad that I was single. At least I didn't have to deal with a drunken abusive twat anymore.

All I had to deal with was the drunken coven, of which, I was a fully-fledged member. Cheers!

Our evening was full of laughter, mainly at the dick pics which they absolutely had to see.

'What in god's name is that?' Rachel stared wide eyed at the screen. She'd obviously been married for too long.

'It's a dick…. I know you've been stuck with the same one for 20 years, but they do come in different shapes and sizes… and in super mushroom shape too, it seems.' Charlotte pointed out.

Our table screeched with laughter. Whoever that floppy fungi belonged to had not wanted to reveal themselves further. And I could see why, poor chap.

The conversation changed to different body sizes. How we were all unhappy with something or wished our *something* was a little bigger, smaller or firmer. It seemed than no matter how beautiful we saw a person; they were unhappy about some part of themselves.

Social media hadn't helped. It had spread false and filtered images around like a virus, creeping into our confidence and attacking it silently. I'd never understood why people used filters to pretend to be flawless, surely, we should embrace every so-called 'flaw'. We should celebrate the shit out of them, it was the only vaccine to that nasty confidence crushing virus.

We'd all become philosophical, and it was time to call it a night.

As was my normal, the moment I got home, the cute clothes came off and the pyjamas went on. Dirty, and slightly drunk mare that I was, I went to bed without bothering to remove my make-up. My head hit the pillow, and I joined in the dogs' snoring.

***

The next morning, I was very glad that the kids had stayed at their friends' houses. A rare and beautiful silence filled the house. Looking in the mirror, Alice Cooper stared back at me. One boob had attempted a great escape from my bra overnight, and my hair was a nest head not seen since my 1980's backcombing obsession.

Gorgeous. Tucking the escapee boob back into place, I headed for the bathroom. I was quite excited about the prospect of having a bath without interruptions.

Arguments usually echoed through the house from the older two, shattering any peace and the youngest child always 'really, *really*' needed a poo whenever I stepped into the soothing waters.

Generally, by the time he was finished, the bath was a tepid offering and I, once again, lamented my lack of funds for a nanny, or boarding school.

I ignored the dog's hints that a walk was overdue and picked up my phone. What had they signed me up for?

I read my profile. Apparently, I was, and I quote *'one hot middle-aged momma who needed a riding partner.'*

I was momentarily confused, whilst I thought horses were okay, I didn't go horse riding….. oh fuck. NO! Gross! Delete, delete, delete.

It wouldn't let me change anything without the password. I couldn't remember the password. What the hell was it? Panic set in.

I rang the non-related sister, 'You set of knobs! What's the password?'

My words were met with her dirty laugh, 'It's funny!'

'It isn't! You're evil! What's the password?'

A minute later, I'd changed the tag line to a more mild-mannered version. Panic over. Or so I thought. My messages were filled with icky responses about jockeys and riding crops.

God, I hoped that no one recognised me.

I was not that lucky it seemed.

There he was, poor Mr Wilson, the hounded art teacher. He was not only on a dating site, but he was on this one and he'd sent a message. I could feel my face burning. I could only imagine the humiliation, the tarring and feathering from the posh lot at the next PTA [which I regularly sent my apologies to for my absence]

What if he told everyone in the staff room? He wouldn't, surely? He'd be admitting he was on a dating site too and that's not something people tend to broadcast, is it?

My heart raced as I opened the message, *"Not quite the description I'd have gone for!"*

What did that mean? Had I just been insulted by the man I'd always felt so sorry for, the man I'd always thought needed protecting from the rubber tit brigade?

The shit.

Well, fuck off Wilson, I hope the plastic piranhas eat you for breakfast.

How was I ever going to live that down?

Date 4

Still sulking and angry about Mr Wilson's statement that I could only assume, meant he didn't think I was hot, I sat hugging a coffee and my bruised ego.

I was hot! Well, maybe more of a tepid most of the time, but there was no need for that response. Little prat.

I distracted myself with tidying up the house. I'd made a bit of a mess shedding clothes like confetti across the bedroom floor. So, my last morning of child freedom was spent picking up after myself before a last-minute arrangement for an early tea with the mothership loomed.

My mum was a force of nature. She was also one of those sly wonders of the world that nothing seemed to escape.

I was greeted with the usual 'I do worry about you Freya; you look a bit haggard.'

'Thanks Mum.' No point in mentioning the dating or Wilson's reply about the level of my 'hot', it would only add fuel to the lecture fire. 'I'm fine, late night with the coven, that's all.'

'Self-inflicted then, no sympathy.' Said the woman who had more than her fair share of party fun.

As older people do, she kindly shared her neighbour's latest medical issues with me [I'm sure Florence would appreciate me knowing all about her IBS]

Somehow, mum seamlessly moved from the topic of IBS to the latest holiday she'd booked. She had several holidays each year, which was great. She'd worked hard all her life, and it was now time to enjoy it.

What got me, was that she always said how skint she was right before telling me how much the latest holiday had cost. It was almost a ritual. She'd lament her pauper status like she was headed for the workhouse in bare feet and rags, and then she'd tell you that she was off to the Maldives or Bali – again.

'If you haven't got the money mum, don't go,' was the only thing I could say.

'Don't be ridiculous darling, of course I've *got* the money, and I deserve a little holiday!'

'You do', I agreed.

'On the subject of money,' she paused.

Oh, bloody hell, had I borrowed a fiver and forgotten to give it back to her?

'I've just put some money in the children's accounts, I thought they might want to get themselves a little treat. I can't imagine their shithead of a father has bothered to give them anything, too busy spending it on that ugly tart of his.' She never missed the opportunity. 'And well, you're not exactly in a position to treat them much, so I've taken care of it.'

'Thanks mum, I'll let them know.' I didn't bother saying I needed a treat too, and after Wilson's put down, I needed a *big* bloody treat.

On the way back to the car, I listened to the usual lecture on my 'potty mouth', which was a bit rich coming from the woman who taught me the delightful profanities in the first place.

We hugged and said goodbye.

***

Still pissed off and horrified at my former dating profile statement, I hadn't bothered checking my messages until I got home. There were a few.

Tom, 45. Fire Co-ordinator [I hoped he wasn't a professional arsonist]

Separated, children, liked Llamas and Pokemon.

I read that twice, Pokemon? Was that code for a kinky sex thing I'd never heard of? Pokey Mon.

Surely, he didn't mean Pikatu and Co? What adult would own up to being obsessed with cartoony fighting animals, especially before you got to know them?

His message confirmed my fears, *"Hey there, hoping my Bulbasaur can Squirtle your Charizard."*
What the actual fuck Tom.

That line had surely never, ever got a positive response of *'Hey babe, my Wigglytuff is just aching for your Jigglypuff.'*

No Tom. No.

Elliot, 50. Paramedic.

Divorced, Camra Member [I hoped this meant the real ale group and not a peeping Tom club]

Oh, and Elliot was a scout leader. Hmm, a scout leader... unwanted memories came flooding back of old Mr Taylor in his scout uniform. His trousers were hoisted so high that his balls were almost in different continents. *shudder*.

Something about Elliot just screamed, nothing coherent, it just screamed. Ignoring wanker Wilson's message still sat there, I moved onto the next message.

Oh, now this looked more promising.

Fernando, 51. Lecturer in history.

Divorced, 1 child. Loved the Greek islands, feta cheese and olives.

Me too Fernando, me too.

Ignoring the fact that I'd started humming the Abba song, I thought Fernando looked rather nice. He had hair.... quite a lot of it going by his profile pic, his arms were extraordinarily hairy. Some of my friends can't stand the overly hairy body but I didn't have a problem with it. It saved on heating bills in winter.

Fernando had a nice smile and had sent a nice message, *"Evening. I think your profile has a lot in common with mine [presuming someone else wrote your tag line though!] and I thought it might be nice to have a chat".*
Harmless, non-offensive, so I replied.
I liked the fact that we could easily chat about history and historical figures. It was nice to be able to talk about literature and the influences of historical events. Boring as it seemed to a lot of people, it was something that I found interesting – just like some people found train spotting interesting, I suppose.
Oh my god, I was a history train spotter.

The conversations led to meeting arrangements and finally, I could look forward to a coffee date and a decent conversation. Huzzah!
With the safety friend in place, I found a seat in the café. Fernando hadn't yet arrived. Ten minutes in and I checked my messages, nothing.
Wondering if there had been a car crunch, I checked the local news, nothing. Likewise, no reports of plagues of locusts or alien invasion. So, I sat and waited, whilst exchanging glances with Charlotte.
After another 20 minutes, I messaged her, *"How long am I supposed to wait before I leave?"*

"Give it ten mins, then fuck it off," was her gracious reply.

Message to Charlotte, *"There's no message from him. Sent one asking if all is well….. nothing back".*

"Hmm, traffic?"

"Maybe." I checked the time; he was 55 minutes late.

I muttered to myself, 'Bollocks to this.'

As I got up to leave and noticed the lady at the counter looking at me with her 'You poor thing, you've been stood up' eyes.

Yes lady. Yes, I fucking well have.

I stomped back to my car with Charlotte jogging after me and checked my messages again. 'That can't be right.'

'What? What's up?' she asked, 'Well, besides being left hanging.'

'His profile isn't there anymore.'

She peered over my shoulder, 'Erm, I think you've been blocked.'

'What? Why? I haven't done anything wrong!' I pathetically protested.

I'd been ghosted. Fucking ghosted. I mean, that's just plain rude. I'd used the decent shampoo and body lotion, only to be ghosted. What a waste of posh products.

'I bet he's married, and she found out.' was the only comfort that she offered, 'Hairy tosser. You'd have been picking those out of your teeth for months.'

I couldn't help but laugh, on the outside.

***

I was in a particularly shit mood that evening. Why would Fernando have done that? Was this all part of the game of online dating? Was there a secret archaic man [or woman] handbook?

Chapter 4, section 5 *"Ghost 'em. Keeps 'em hanging, makes 'em eager for contact, don't you know."*

Well Fernando, you can take chapter 4, section 5 and stick it right up your…. I didn't finish that thought as my phone pinged. Expecting Fernando and a huge gushing apology, I opened the app.

To my horror, it was wanker Wilson.

"How are things? You sifting through the drongo's ok? It's worse for blokes, you wouldn't believe the desperate housewives and ego's on here."

What? Did he want my sympathy? Against my better judgement and mainly because I was angry that my ego had taken a bit of a bashing, I replied. *"TBH, it's a bit shit. Got ghosted today."*

"Yeah, that happens. Don't take it personally. Probably married and got caught."

And offline he went. Right. Thanks for that gem of an insight Wilson.

Was online dating as tough for men as it was for women? I hadn't really given it much thought. I'd known a few women that had been really pissed around and hurt by people they were dating. I'd also worked with a few women who thought it was amusing to be total bitches and brag about treating someone badly.

It seemed to me that it didn't matter who you were, or who you were looking for, some people were just plain nasty. The tough part of life was not letting the nasty change you into a seething pile of revenge and venom.

Then of course, there were all the fake bits to get through. The false eyelashes and hair dye were almost expected as everyday additions to people's outfits, like jewellery, but what about the pumped-up lips, hair extensions and chicken fillets. I'd often wondered how guys felt about all of that. Was it like false advertising? Or was it just accepted that it came as part of the dating armour?

The sadness was that most people looked far more beautiful without surgical enhancements.

'Yeah, I bet fucking Fernando would've turned up if I'd have been enhanced,' I murmured to my growing self-pity.

As I was still reeling from Fernando's ghosting, I couldn't help it, I searched 'Why do people ghost you on dating apps?'.

Staring me in the face [according to Google] was the reason. *"Most people ghost due to their own shortcomings. Unfortunately, it can trigger feelings of rejection and a need to seek revenge in the person being ghosted"*

And there it was. Wanker Wilson was right, although I didn't want to admit it…. I shouldn't take it personally.

Fernando obviously had 'shortcomings' and I was sure as shit, not going to let it trigger feelings of rejection or revenge.

I simply wished Fernando a nasty bout of diarrhoea in a very public place.

Date 5

After a crappy weekend, I really wanted a decent day at work, but no. Monday morning came with 2 hours of menopause training.

The future had never looked so gloomy than after that training. It seemed what was lying in wait for women when it hit, was moods, sweats and a dry vagina.

Mine probably had more cobwebs than an abandoned shed, and certainly less visitors. In addition, all it had to look forward to was the consistency of sandpaper. Awesome.

I messaged the coven. I really needed a silly zoom call to cheer me up. Once the kids were safely out of earshot in their rent-free hovels, I joined the call.

I spilled the beans on the arid future of their personal areas and then off-loaded the humiliation of ghosty Fernando and then wanker Wilson's comment over the 'hot middle-aged' line.

The overwhelming response was that Fernando was indeed a tosser and Wilson couldn't have meant to insult.

Apparently, 'I'd been over-sensitive and taken it the

wrong way.'

Over-sensitive indeed! As if I was EVER over-sensitive. Rude.

Charlotte was still having a great time juggling her dates from various dating sites. Apparently, it was totally fine to keep your options open if you're honest about still window shopping. Fair enough.

She mentioned the mixer. I'd ignored the email from admin, so I'd no idea what the mixer was.

'What's a mixer? Not a kitchen blender obviously! What is it?' Rachel, like me was clueless.

Charlotte explained.

A mixer, it seemed, was a regular meet-up of those on the dating site. Arranged by admin, you could view the goods on offer in person.

Rachel, innocent in many things said, 'A bit like a horrible cattle market, where you view the living meat before you send it to slaughter?'

Charlotte nodded, 'Exactly.'

Sounded interesting, 'Okay, it might be exactly what I need, rate before you date! I'm in!'

In a profile, people lie about all sorts of things including physical appearance but in person, you couldn't suddenly grow 6 inches and gain a personality.

If wanker Wilson was to be believed, that goes for women too. A mixer could just be the way forward, so it was agreed, the mixer it was.

It was arranged for the following weekend. I'd even made an appointment at the hairdressers to have my locks [well, frizz] sorted out. With something to look forward to other than bickering kids and drooling dogs, I found myself humming away at work and even did a little happy dance in the foyer. On CCTV, it probably looked like I was trying to escape a wasp, but I was in a good mood and didn't care.

I'd mainly pre-selected my outfit and even bought some decent underwear, no grey bobbly bra for me. However, the hairdresser pamper experience was not as I'd hoped. She picked up my hair, pulled a face like someone had farted, and then muttered about how fine it was.

Yes lady, I have a lot of hair. A lot of fine, disappointingly frizzy hair. Drop the judgement and just do your thing, I'm paying you handsomely to make me look like a glossy Rapunzel.

She tried her best anyway.

***

After two hissy fits, a heap of discarded dresses and a vague grunt of approval from my daughter, I got in the taxi and went to collect my non-related sister.

'Woah, you look sooo nice.'

The way she said it implied that this was indeed a rare thing, and that was probably true. I'd never been one for sticking a full face of make-up on for the school drop off or for work. I was more of an 'I'll do' person. If I was clean, I didn't need to be overly tidy, did I?

Also, I quite liked the way I felt when I did put in the effort. It made me feel like I could be seen and that felt good.

I returned the compliment. 'Well, *Lottie the hottie*, you look awesome. I'm not standing next to you, you bitch!'

Charlotte was rattling off a list of names of people who had said they would be there. Just how she was going to sift through these, was a mystery but she seemed very confident.

As she should, she was a successful therapist, something that I found quite ironic, given her serial dating habits and her crackers friend group. She was stunning, funny and seemingly immune to negativity. That's not to say it didn't hurt her, many a teary evening and boxes of tissues were evidence of that, but she had the capability of turning shit situations into incredible adventures. I envied her for that.

As had already been pointed out, I could be a bit oversensitive.

Balloons had been slapped all over the entrance to the venue to form a wonky arch. I hated balloons. Constantly threatening to explode. Kids' parties were a hideous experience. All those chubby hands squeezing them. I swear kids could feel my terror and taunted me with each nip and flick of that stretched latex.

Ignoring the balloons, we entered the cattle market. Charlotte walked in with such confidence that she could have been attending the premier of her own hit movie.

I kind of trailed in with a smile that said I had wind. She plonked the ugly name tag unceremoniously on my boob, I moved it. I didn't really want the eyes of all the bargain hunters to use the name tag as an excuse to stare at the chesticles.

And the judgement began. Men hunted for their prey. Women glared at their competition, and I headed for the bar. It was cheaper to buy a bottle of wine than two separate glasses, I never understood the justification of that, but cheaper worked for me.

As we headed for a spare table, I could feel the laser eyes piercing my make-up armour. I hadn't even sat down when one came straight in for the kill.

'Hi luv, I'm Greg,' unnecessarily Greg pointed to his name tag which was hanging like a threat on his overly small t-shirt.

I hated being called 'luv'; it grated on me like a cheap body scrub.

'Evening,' I tried to give him the polite 'This conversation is going no further' brush off.

Greg ignored that and attempted to glue himself to my side, his balding head already gleaming with sweat. My non-related sister stopped Greg from sitting down.

'This seat's taken. Nice to meet you though.' She brushed him off like a pro. Awesome.

Then it began, Charlotte pointed out her hopefuls, '2 o'clock, that's Josh. He is the one I really like. 4 o'clock in the white t-shirt, that's Shay. He's lovely but it's not going to work, he's a bit needy.' She paused for a drink, 'Oh and 6'oclock, that's Aaron, funny as fuck.'

I looked at the man-clock like an MI6 spy. Sneaking a peak like a pro, I nodded approval at Josh and tried to avoid eye contact with the two guys who had evidently never seen a spy movie. Openly ogling was more their MO.

Marcus and his mate, Kayzo tried their luck next.

Sadly, as nice as Marcus seemed, he really should have stayed away from the garlic. His breath lingered in the air for a good ten minutes after he left. I dabbed my watering eyes and ignored the glare of the woman in the red dress, who obviously thought Marcus was there for her.

All yours sweetheart, if you can handle that garlic cloud, you've earned him.

The next intake of arrivals wandered through, all eyes on them, including mine. I marvelled at just how quickly I had joined the hunt. My eyes rested on one very familiar figure.

I elbowed my non-related sister, 'That's fucking Fernando. Cheeky bastard! He ghosted me and then turns up to the mixer.'

'Bastard.' She agreed.

His hairy arms poked out from his rolled-up sleeves, he saw me and veered off into the crowd. Arsehole.

I was dragged from my brewing anger by the need to pee. As I headed for the bathroom, I smiled without directly looking at the sea of equally hopeful and hostile eyes.

The women's bathroom is a hotbed of tears, tantrums and gossip. Women, especially drunk women, are totally hilarious… and bloody bitchy.

I listened to the conversations about "her in that dress who thinks she can pull anyone" and the note-sharing on various guys they had dated.

The trick is, that when washing your hands or reapplying your make-up, you smile and stay silent. They don't seem to notice you.

Never skipping a beat at my sudden appearance, the three women were happily dissecting their victims.

'Charlie's got a dick the size of Australia, but it stinks of brie, and he couldn't find his way around a woman's body with a sat nav.'

Good to know. Avoid Charlie.

'That twat ghosted me. ME! How dare he, as if he was gonna get a shag anyway.'

Not Fernando, but at least I wasn't the only one being ghosted, it made me feel momentarily better.

'He is *gorgeous!* He's been checking me out, I mean, why wouldn't he!'

Woah! Ego lady.

'Did you see her dress? It's gorgeous, but it looks shit on her.'

I hoped they weren't talking about me.

The journey back to my seat was uneventful. People seemed to be grouping or coupling up. Had I missed my opportunity?

Charlotte was happily chatting to a couple of guys, one of which I noted was Mr 2 o'clock, Josh. She had kindly replenished the wine stocks, so I sat and tried not to look like Tommy-no-mates.

Fernando had disappeared, as he should, in shame. I was beginning to think that the evening was a waste of time when I sensed someone standing next to me.

'Hi, can I sit here?'

Ooooh, polite and not bad looking at all. I agreed that Mr blue jeans could sit down.

Craig, 43. Gardener and lover of the great outdoors.

I could see that from his tan line peeking out from the sleeve of his t-shirt. His comments about it being a cattle market in there made me think, that like me, he was a bit out of his comfort zone.

A fan of action films and Peter Kay, Craig chatted away happily, even loosely suggesting a meet up sometime. Ok, this was going well. My non-related sister was keeping a watchful eye out and winked, evidently approving of Craig.

He went to the bar, and she immediately took his place.

'Nice.'

'Yeah, he seems to be. He's asked lots of questions and made me laugh a few times.'

'And he's tall, bonus!' She breezed off to her audience.

Craig came back with some kind of cocktail. I thought it was for me and was about to point out the bottle of wine sat on the table, when he started drinking it. Oh. Ok. Nothing wrong with a man who drinks cocktails, it works for James Bond.

It was at this point that Craig asked me how old I was. No point in lying, why would I? I'm not trying to be something I'm not. So, I told him.

To say that he looked startled was an understatement. He almost poked himself in the eye with the little cocktail umbrella and spluttered, 'Oh, Christ. I didn't know you were that old, I thought you were more my age. You're too old for me. Sorry.'

And off he went, into the crowd, ending my night with another smack in the ego. I sat holding my glass, wondering what the fuck just happened.

Charlotte disengaged herself from her fan club as the taxi arrived and I offloaded the sorry saga in the taxi, 'I didn't have the chance to say anything to him, he just pissed off after that,' my chin wobbled as I held back the tears.

'Look, at least he was honest,' was her attempt at comforting me, 'and it saves you wasting your time.'

After that she delivered the tirade, 'What a wanker! Saying that, right to your fucking face. I mean, you don't look 50 fucking 3!'

The pity in the taxi driver's eyes didn't help.

Back to the drawing board.

Date 6

I felt, well, I don't quite know what. Had I been made to feel embarrassed about my age or had I done that to myself? Had my reaction to Craig's evident shock at my years, caused this feeling of 'am I just too old for this?'

I look at my friends, and they're the same as they always were. That's because we are ageing together, as one. Here's the thing, I'm bloody grateful to be ageing, some people never get the chance to and I'm lucky to have been given the chance to age. So why was I suddenly very self-conscious of my decades?

Yeah, yeah. With age comes wisdom, mostly, although that's very questionable for some people. The only wisdom they have is their teeth.

With age comes experience, and not all experiences are ever worth repeating but I suddenly felt like shit because I was born 53 bloody years ago.

I looked in the mirror [which is not always my friend] and gave myself a bit of a pep talk.

'You're not too old! You've just had a bunch of [not very big] pricks in your life. This isn't on you. It's on them!'

By the time my pep talk was over, I knew it was Craig's problem, not mine. I just didn't fit his list was all.

Still feeling crappy, I messaged the coven.

"Fuck him" was their response, *"He sounds like an arse."*

Yep, Craig, you're an arse.

My phone pinged and I groaned. Wanker Wilson has sent a message, *"Did you enjoy the mixer?"*

What? He wasn't there, how the hell did he know I'd been? His message was a question, he was expecting a reply.

I was weary and felt somewhat crone-like, so he got the full-on honest reply. *"Not really. It was like being judged by a set of ageist wankers, slappers and dick wads."*

Make of that what you will Wilson.

He didn't reply and I didn't care.

***

At work, the IT had been absolutely crap for months and today was the so called 'big fix'. We all had to work from home while they sorted the system out. Jeremy, head of IT, was on the case. We couldn't Teams or use our work phones due to the whole system being offline.

I'd given him my personal mobile number and joked that I didn't want it signed up to free samples of pile cream.

I wasn't sure he got my sense of humour because he simply responded with, 'Of course not.'

Trying to create a last-minute report with no accessible data was a bloody joke but I persevered and cursed my lack of using a pen for so long. My hand cramped like a bored wankers', so I opted for a heap of toast and marmite instead.

My phone rang, gah! A video call. Jeremy. Momentary panic. I'd not even bothered to get dressed properly and still had my pyjamas on. Fuck.

Wiping the marmite string from my chin, I answered. Jeremy appeared on screen.

Ooooh, well, hello to you Jeremy!

Although I'd spoken to him on various occasions, I'd never seen the guy before. I knew that because I would have remembered that particular Gerard Butler look-a-like.

Please, please, please don't let me look like a pyjama trog. I tried my very best smile, but the little picture in the corner told me that I'd gone for constipated instead.

Jeremy was all business, 'the fibre this, the meta that'. I paid very little attention. I was just happy to watch him talk.

I realised that Jeremy had finished talking and was obviously waiting for a response. Shit.

'Sorry Jeremy, it's terrible reception here. Can you just say that again please?'

'I just asked if you'd received the pile cream yet?'

'Erm, ha, erm,' any witty retort got lost between my brain and my gob. I resembled a goldfish. Awesome.

'Anyway, it should all be working now. Give me a call if there are any problems. And,' he hesitated, 'if you fancy going for a drink sometime, you've got my number.'

A drink? Holy crap, had he just asked me out on a date? Quick. Engage brain.

'Thank you. Yeah, that would be nice. Just let me know when for drinks. And you've got my number too, pile cream, so call me.'

Yep, cool as a cucumber….. that's been left out of the fridge in 100-degree heat. Smashing.

Immediately, I notified the coven. I'd been asked on a date, a real live date.

"Woo feckin hoo," was the collective response.

How long should I leave it. Would he contact me? I'd said that he should let me know when, so it was up to him, surely?

That evening, there was nothing from Jeremy. A bit deflated, I decided to poke around the dating site, check out messages and generally have a good old nosey at some profiles.

One profile I hadn't looked at was wanker Wilson's. If I looked at his profile, would it notify him? A quick Google told me that people were only notified if you 'liked' their profile, I was safe, there's no way I was 'liking' his profile. Confident that he wouldn't think I was a stalker, I viewed Wilson's profile.

Zak, 35.

Hmmm, I hadn't got him pegged as a Zak and I wasn't sure it suited him. At 35 he was a baby, only just out of the embryo stage to an old hag like me. [Yes, I was still bitter about the age thing]

I stared at the screen, he'd put himself down as an artist and an educator, fair enough, he was an art teacher.

He had kids and was a widower.

I'm not sure what shocked me more, the fact that he had kids or that he'd lost his wife. Perhaps it was because he was so young, far too young to have faced such tragedy, that's for sure.

I viewed his profile and felt a bit ashamed. I'd been a bit of a bitch to wan... to Wilson.

Or had I? Surely, I couldn't have overreacted.

I had and I knew it.

He liked the natural world as it influenced his art. There were also 2 other photos of him looking chilled and relaxed, without a hint of his teacher's shirt and tie.

I felt guilty for poking around his profile, I went to log out and stop the prying.

He messaged. *"A dick wad? Made me laugh. I'm going try to get that into conversation in the staff room, 3 points to me if I do!"*

I laughed. That's the kind of thing that the coven did, word of the day and points for slipping it unnoticed into conversations.

I replied, *"Try knob sack. It's harder to slip in [no pun intended] 5 points for that one!"*

My phone told me I'd got a text. All thoughts of Wilson and the quest I'd just sent him on, forgotten.

It was Jeremy, *"You free tonight or tomorrow to grab that drink?"*

Blimey, he was keen.

Mr Gerard Butler look-a-like, tomorrow is good.

This time, because I knew [of] Jeremy from work, I didn't feel the need for a safety friend. We were going for grown-up drinks too, no coffee breath for me this time!

***

I waited in a bar that I knew from work do's and felt quite comfortable with the familiar layout. I'd already sat at the best table so that I could view the door. I'd arrived early, firstly because I can't stand being late for anything and secondly, because it meant he would have to walk in and look for me.

When people are looking for someone, they tend to, without realising it, look totally gormless. I didn't want to look gormless, so I chose the early arrival.

Jeremy waltzed in and, on time too. I couldn't miss him… or the god-awful Hawaiian shirt he'd chosen to wear.

Christ alive, we weren't on a bloody cruise. The yellow flowery shirt headed my way and plopped down in the chair opposite me, 'Hey, what are you drinking?'

Okay, I could look past the shirt [with sunglasses] I made my order and waited for him to return.

Jeremy chatted about IT hell, it was after all, the one thing we knew that we had in common. I steered the conversation away from work and found out he was a HUGE baseball fan. Fuck. I knew nothing about baseball and that disappointed him.

'That's a shame. You should watch some games, you might not understand the rules, most women don't, but the games are great.'

A light went out in my eyes, 'You never know, I might surprise you and understand the rules! Stranger things have happened.'

'I doubt it.' He smiled politely.

Strike 1.

Jeremy loved holidays to Benidorm. And not the old town. Tales of him and his 'posse' as he called them, filled the next 15 minutes. Grabbing passing tits was the general entertainment. Yards of beer [and puke] were apparently, a must.

'You shoulda seen Becker, right after he stuck his face in her norks, he puked a rainbow!'

He, at least, found that amusing.

Strike 2.

I went to the bar to grab another round to numb the pain. When I got back, Jeremy had moved seats so that he could lean against the wall and sat directly under wall light. He began yet another tale of drunken lads' holidays and boob ogling.

It was then that I'd looked up at him and nearly spat a gob full of Pinot Grigio everywhere. His head was threadbare. Fuckin threadbare. Like an old rug that had lost its shag pile. I could see all the way through to his scalp.

Confused, I tried for a closer look. He mistook it for me moving in for a kiss. One bumped forehead later, I realised that his scalp had been covered with some kind of dark product. He'd sprayed it to make it look like he had a thick thatch of hair, when in fact he had less hair than a freshly waxed arse crack.

Strike 3 and out.

If a bloke is bald, or balding, they should wear it with pride. Just because I don't find it attractive, doesn't mean a thing. There are gazillions of women out there who like [and even prefer] a baldy, but for the love of god, don't spray your noggin and try to pass it off as actual hair.

Luckily, I didn't work with Jeremy in any capacity other than remotely. And that's how it would remain. He never contacted me again other than to announce a software update, which I ignored.

'Maybe I'm just not meant to date,' was becoming my pathetic mantra.

Even my non-related sister seemed to have decided upon Mr 2 o'clock, forsaking all others. I couldn't even get a second coffee date, never mind narrowing it down from four hopefuls to one solo contender.

I spent the next couple of weeks declaring that I was done with the whole dating bollocks, although I never deleted my profile.

Well, you never know, do you?

Date 7

Being a crappy light sleeper was a curse. I swear I could hear a gnat fart a mile away, and my neighbours' motorbike was way louder than a gnat at 4.30am. The dogs looked hopeful as I got up and yanked on the jogging bottoms.

Early morning dog walks meant that I lobbed on the nearest clothes [usually mismatched] had a piddle and set off. The hairbrush wasn't even a thought.

I loved the early morning walks. No one was ever around, and I could have conversations with the dogs and off-load all my worries onto two creatures that would never judge me.

In addition, one of my dogs was an anti-social prat. He had a history of making a total knob of himself every time another dog was within 50 meters. Quite frankly, it was just embarrassing. Walking knob-dog looked like I was trying to hang onto a team of dragons with a feather. So, I preferred early morning and late-night walks.

I'd headed over the field towards the tall fence, trying [and failing] to stop knob-dog from eating horse shit.

'Christ, you dirty sod! Don't you come near me with your shit breath. No! I don't want kisses.'

'Glad to hear it. I wouldn't want to share my shit breath with you anyway.'

Startled, I spun round. Wilson, dressed in shorts and a t-shirt was ambling along the other side of the fence with, what can only be described as, a rat on a lead. Knob-dog immediately thought it was breakfast time.

My other dog wanted to play. The rat on a lead had started yapping like its life depended on it. Knob-dog reacted, tried to jump the fence and pulled me straight down, flat on my face.

'Enough,' Wilson said firmly.

Knob-dog and the yapping rat both stopped immediately. [It was only well after the fact that I was vaguely impressed by that.]

'Are you alright?' He peered through the 8-foot metal fence like a pervert at a peep show.

I gasped for air and could only manage a thumbs up whilst secretly promising knob-dog that he was going straight to the sausage factory.

Knob-dog sat perfectly still, like butter wouldn't melt. I glared at him with undisguised loathing.

'You've got mud on your chin. Or at least I hope it's mud!' Wilson seemed amused.

I was not amused, not in the slightest. Humiliated, yes, but amused? Not one fucking bit.

I wiped my chin on an equally dirty arm. 'Morning. I've added gymnastics into the daily exercise.'

'I think a bit more practice on the gymnastics is needed.' Wilson laughed and wandered off with the rat on a lead into the trees.

All the way home I chuntered to the knob-dog. He didn't care about the chaos he'd caused, nor that his breath smelt like arses.

One shower later, with a coffee in hand, I enjoyed the peace of the morning. The kids were still sleeping [of course] I closed my eyes and replayed the stunning events of the morning.

I'd never wanted the dogs. They had officially belonged my [former] husband. He'd left without them when he got caught playing 'poke the pussy' with his off-brand Kardashian. So, by default, just like the kids, they became my sole responsibility.

The phone ping broke my brewing bitterness at both ex-husband and knob-dog. I hoped it wasn't Wilson taking the piss out of my lost dignity.

It wasn't Wilson. It was a very generous offer from **Fred, 72**.

Fred [retired police sergeant] was proposing to give me a thorough working over and even had his handcuffs at the ready.

Fuck off Fred, you'll pop a hip.

I realised at that point that I hadn't checked any messages for the past couple of weeks, not that my inbox was bursting with exciting propositions. I'd missed Wilson's claim of 5 points for getting 'knob-sack' into conversation with Mr Reeder, the geography teacher.

Good for you, Wilson. I didn't reply. I couldn't be arsed.

The other messages were a mixed bunch.

Matt, 53. Librarian.

Hmm, I knew some librarians. Matt was either going to be Dirk Dullard or a secret Lively Leonard. There seemed to be no middle ground with the librarians that I'd met.

Matt had put his relationship status as 'It's complicated'. According to Charlotte, that was code for 'bored at home and want a fling'.

Nope, not even delving into that, thank you.

David, 51. Gynaecologist.

Urgh, no thanks. I could only imagine the conversation over dinner, 'How was your day darling?'

'Great, I checked out 14 fannies' today.'

Somehow, I imagined that dating a gynaecologist would feel like he'd been on a car comparison website all day, and you'd always wonder how your vehicle stacked up.

Good luck David. May your days be filled with marvellous muffs.

Harry, 54. Banker and self-confessed nerd.

Loved good food and decent wine. He'd put something amusing about a mosh pit at a Metallica gig which hit a chord.

I'd been smashed in the nose by an over excited 'friend' at a Metallica gig as a teenager. When James Hetfield appeared, she went bananas…. and my nose went… banana shaped. I'd never forgiven that cow bag. We hadn't spoken for 35 years but the bump on my nose reminded me almost daily of how much I hated her.

However, Harry seemed like an interesting prospect. His list of dislikes was similar and included noisy eaters, bad breath [note to self: always carry Polos] and one-sided conversations.

We spent most of the evenings chatting via messages and a few calls, he had a welcome seductive tone to his voice. To my delight, a date was arranged for the following weekend.

The kids began to suspect that I was up to something.

'Who's messaging you?' my daughter asked.

I diverted attention by offering a takeaway.

That did the trick on Lexi, but my son, Cal, wasn't having any of it. 'Well, someone's making you laugh, for a change. You're normally well moody.'

Cheeky little shitehawk.

Saturday arrived and I was SO looking forward to meeting Harry in person. I had high hopes for this date and chose, what I thought, was a flattering dress and my nice heels.

My youngest son, Finn, sat on the sofa and told me I looked 'special'.

I took that as a compliment.

Cal looked me up and down, looked across at his twin sister and had the gall to say, 'Told you! She's going on an old people's date.'

She replied with, 'Urgh, cringe.'

There are times that I really disliked my older offspring and wondered why I didn't sell them on eBay.

'Actually,' big fat half-lie alert, 'I'm meeting your aunties for a nice drink to get away from you lot of smelly poops.'

The babysitter eyed me suspiciously.

Don't judge me lady, you've already eaten half of the kids' biscuits and blamed it on the dogs.

***

I arrived at the pub hoping that I wasn't overdressed, it wasn't exactly the swankiest of places, but at least my feet weren't sticking to the carpet. I got my white wine, which tasted more like white vinegar [note to self: steer clear of house white] nodded to Sarah and Rachel, who had volunteered for the safety friend roles for the evening, and waited eagerly for Harry.

Harry arrived…. with a mate. Okay, maybe he felt he needed a safety friend too. Women could be serial killers as much as men, the double deviant they were known as. Thankfully, he left his mate at the bar and came over.

Harry was really good looking in a non-classical Hollywood way, and I liked that. Chiselled jaws, waxed eyebrows and perfects tans were not for me.

We pretty much picked up the conversation where we'd left it the night before, and I had a really good feeling about him.

I went to grab more drinks, and he stood up. 'Fuckin' hell, you're tall.'

'Erm, not really. I'm only 5' 8".' I smiled awkwardly. What did he mean? Yeah, with heels, I'm taller but I'm no Amazonian goddess.

At the bar I couldn't help but wonder what the hell that was about. He didn't say it in an admiringly, it was more of a vaguely horrified statement. I turned around and he was staring in a way that made me feel like I was being scanned at an airport security check-in.

I went back to my seat, very self-conscious of how I walked. Heel to toe, don't trip up. Relax the shoulders, straighten that back.

As I sat back down and passed him his pint, he leaned in. 'Look, I know we get on, like personality wise.'

I felt the 'but' before it came, and I don't mean I felt his arse.

'But…. I have to be honest. You're too tall and too

kind of, whatever, for me to find, you know, physically attractive,' he started waffling awkwardly, 'there's got to be a physical spark hasn't there and as nice as you are,' Harry took a huge gulp of his lager before delivering the final blow, 'I'm sorry, but you're just the wrong…. shape.'

My mouth opened like a frog. 'What do you mean, the wrong shape?'

'You know what I mean. I just prefer women who are, bigger, you know, got something on them to grab hold of. You looked bigger in your photo. Sorry. Please don't be offended.'

Offended? Too right I'm offended Harry. I'm aggrieved, affronted, insulted and FUCKING OFFENDED.

He collected his mate from the bar and disappeared into the night.

I gathered my safety friends and cried all the way to the taxi rank.

'The physical spark for Harry was more of a dud firework on a soggy Bonfire night…. because I'm the wrong shitty shaped firework,' I wailed.

Rachel, who was normally quite reserved, turned into Samuel L. Jackson on overdrive 'Motherfucker. Mother fuckin fucker.'

Indeed.

Date 8

I had to admit, that hurt. It really, really hurt. I began to wonder if it was payback for my own list of 'requirements'.

Was this the universes' way of telling me that I had no right to even have a list? Like a 'who do you think you are?' but without the family history research?

I spent the rest of the weekend overcompensating. I spent money I didn't have, cried into my pillow more times than I cared to admit and called upon the support of the coven. Of course, they all called the shit out of Harry and his declaration that I was 'the wrong shape.' What the fuck did that even mean?

Yeah, we all like different physiques but my profile pic showed what shape I was. He knew what shape I was from the photos, I was just 'me shaped' and that apparently wasn't right for Harry. Not a lot I could do about that.

Monday evening came around and it was game night. Cal's football team had an inter-school's game. So, I dragged my sorry wrong sized arse to it, and feigned enthusiasm at the prospect of game winning. Standing on the sideline, I looked at all the pristine parents who'd turned up.

I bet they were the right fuckin shape.

The sports teacher, Mr Gilmore was yelling at the team and jumping along the sidelines like an oversized kangaroo. He barged into me and yelled at the team, 'Come on lads, that's it!'.

Had the man no manners?

'Really? I'm bloody deaf in that ear now.' I scowled at him.

The cheeky bastard looked at me and said, 'If you're deaf in that ear, it won't matter if I shout now, will it?'

Twat.

He carried on with his marsupial moves like I wasn't even there. I burst into tears and walked away from the pitch.

They won the game. Hoo fucking rah.

My son chanted the team mantra over and over again, all the way home. I tried to be all cheery and happy for the little weasels. I really did.

***

I laid in the biggest bubble bath that I could without flooding the bathroom. My phone pinged. Dating site message. Oh, fuck off.

As my relaxation CD had told me to do, I put my head under the water and stayed there. The world was a warm and wonderful place, and I was…. No, it was no good, I needed oxygen.

I sat up, coughed, spluttered and dribbled down my chin. Classy.

Once I could breathe again, I looked at my message.

Wilson, *"Hey, you ok? Andy said you looked upset."*

Andy? Who the frig was Andy? I toned it down to a more polite *"Yeah thanks. Who's Andy?"*

As we'd never had an actual real-time exchange, I wasn't expecting a reply, but he pinged one straight back, *"Andy Gilmore, the sports teacher."*

So that was his name, Andy.

Rude twat suited him better.

"Right. He's a rude tosser." I pressed send without really registering who I was talking to.

I panicked, there was no way to cancel the message. Crap.

Wilson didn't reply. I'd obviously gone a step too far and offended his bestie.

A visit from my non-related sister changed the evening's focus. She had dumped Mr 2 o'clock, Josh.

The situation called for more than tea and sympathy, one look at her aunty Charlotte and Lexi went into action, 'Shall I get you some wine?' she whispered.

That girl of mine had been taught well, 'Yes please, I think she needs it.' I winked at her.

It turned out that Josh wasn't all that nice after all. He'd waited until she'd released all surplus candidates into the arms of others, and then revealed that he was actually and in fact, a bit of a wanker.

Josh had displayed what she termed as 'classic coercive' tendencies. He'd convinced her that he was 'the one' and she should drop all other prospects. Which she believed and duly did.

Apparently, he then suggested that ALL she needed was him and her friends [the coven] were surplus to requirements. Her alarm bells rang like a nuclear assault warning.

When confronted with this theory, Josh went all Rambo on her, shooting his gun-mouth off like crazy. She ended it.

All I could say was, 'What a shit! You've had a narrow escape. You're worth more. Hell, You're L'Oreal!'

She signed, 'Yeah, I am' then with more conviction, 'Yes, I fucking am L'Oreal. You know, the minute I stuck with him; I just knew I'd made a mistake.'

I booked a last-minute leave day from work. She needed me more than the research project did. Three glasses of wine later and she declared the need for a break from dating. But seemed eager to push me right back into it.

'C'mon, let's have a look at who's out there.' She grabbed my phone and began sweeping through the profiles.

Al, 52. Zoologist. Lover of log cabins and had a burning desire for exciting 'adventures' that involved several people at once.

The only burning a person would get from that Al, is cystitis.

Al was evidently also a fan of marshmallows, so much so that he resembled one. A pink pudgy face smiled out of his profile pic.

Nope! Al was not for me. I was a one-person person and not a fan of cystitis or marshmallows.

Craig, 43. Still there and probably still making women feel like crap about their age. Turd.

Then, she got giddy, 'Ooooh, he's nice.' Charlotte poked the phone under my nose.

Of course, she'd stopped on Wilson's profile.

'That's Wilson, *The* Wilson.' I expected her to spill some profanities, instead she just made a 'Mmmmm' noise and carried on scrolling. Then she started to laugh.

I knew that laugh all too well, 'What have you just done?'

'I haven't done anything. Honestly. Chill! What about him?' She again stuck my phone in front of my face.

I tried to focus and had to sit back. The blurred face came together to form one good looking chap indeed. I flicked through his pictures with my glasses on, which only improved the view.

Darren, 56. Solicitor, divorced. Darren claimed to like good restaurants and go-karting…. Erm, ok.

Darren disliked subtitles and goats.

I wasn't sure if he was being random in some kind of attempt to be quirky, or if he was a bit of a knob. Hard to tell from a profile. So, I [or the wine I'd guzzled] messaged him.

"I challenge you to a go-karting race, loser buys the drinks."

An hour later, Darren had accepted the challenge, and we arranged the meet.

I woke up the next morning and I was momentarily confused. Why had I got an email with tickets to 'Go Race Em'…. Then I realised why.

Oh shit.

'You've got to go! You challenged him!' My new sofa dweller announced, the empty bottles still sat on the floor.

'Oh, fuck it.' I shrugged.

What had I got to lose. Maybe spontaneous was what I needed. I got ready and headed out with my hangover shouting 'Idiot' as loud as it could.

When we arrived at the aptly named 'Go Race 'Em', Charlotte headed to the café for coffee supplies. I sat feeling rough, wondering if he would show up.

And show up he did. A hello from him and I was lost for words…. And not in a good way.

Either I'd had the WORST case of beer goggles, or his profile pics were VERY heavily photoshopped. The man looked like a giant toddler in dungarees. To make matters worse [if that was possible] his child-like attire was covered in little pictures of go-karts. Was I still pissed?

'Fuck me, what's that?'

The reaction of my non-related sister told me that she was similarly afflicted.

I tried to hide behind the giant coffee she had brought.

Oblivious to our horror and eager to start, he politely said, 'Shall we?'

He indicated towards the holding area for karts. I couldn't run away like some milk sop; I nodded and followed the man-child.

Of course, he had his own personal kart there, why wouldn't he….

I pulled on the suspiciously smelly helmet that I'd been unceremoniously handed, and just prayed that the last wearer hadn't got head lice.

With his cheeks [face, not butt] squished by helmet padding, he indicated that we were doing 3 laps around the track.

His next gesture told me that I was going down, and not in the dominant porno type of going down. He was very determined to win. So much so that his fists pumped the air, and he made some kind of guttural sound. A bit like a gorilla with belly ache.

Reminiscent of Penelope Pitstop being chased by the Hooded Claw[er] I bombed around shouting 'Help, Help' as my little kart hurtled towards the barrier.

Needless to say, I lost the racing challenge.

I managed to untangle one wobbly leg from the kart and Darren, hero that he was, came over to gloat.

'Ha! Loser.' He even added the loser dance for effect.

What were we, 5? Wanker.

I could only hope that Darren was a little more mature at work, I doubt a judge would appreciate the loser dance in the courtroom.

As promised, I provided Darren with the winners' drink…. My stone-cold coffee, and we left.

Charlotte couldn't stop laughing, she howled all the way back to the car. Rotten cow.

***

That afternoon, I stood naked from the waist up in the breast clinic whilst the mammographer slapped my right boulder on the plate like an 18-ounce steak and squished it within an inch of its life.

I sighed. The only action my boobs had seen in the past three years was a soddin mammogram.

Great.

Date 9

My mother had called and invited me to a last-minute leisure and spa weekend. For a [very] brief moment, I felt honoured. Then, she told me that she'd won the break in the church fundraiser and had already asked everyone else, but they were busy, so I was the last [and only] option left.

The weekend was non-refundable [I couldn't believe that she had tried to cash it in] and the date was fixed. So, she was asking me 'out desperation', rather than lose it.

Brilliant. A weekend with the mothership ahoy.

With the kids and dogs farmed out to Sarah and emergency numbers in place, I packed for what was sure to be a memorable time….

I'd no idea what to expect so had covered all bases. Swimming costume, bikini, joggers, jeans and a couple of tops.

Shit! I needed to sort the bikini line out. The last time I took any notice of the Kate, I'd had to tuck the spiders' legs poking out of my knickers, back in.

20 minutes and half a tube of hair remover later, I was good to go, or so I thought.

Quick call from mum, 'Freya, don't forget, I've booked dinner at Restaurant Divinite tonight. Bring something nice, they don't let slobs in.'

The way she pronounced the restaurant's name made her sound like she had a huge gob of phlegm in her throat.

We hadn't even set off and she was already on one. Joy.

Two hours of listening to who won what at the church auction [apparently Margaret Thompson had out-bid mum for the dual spa and beauty package] and my head was ready to explode.

'Margaret fucking Thompson needs more than a beauty package, ugly old trout.'

Blimey, mum was *really* bitter about losing that one.

My attempt to pacify went down like a turd in a swimming pool, 'Well, it's all for charity isn't it. At least they made some decent money.'

'Decent money? Her money comes from her husband's bloody dodgy dealings, back handers I heard. AND as for the vicar's wife, God forgive me,' she held her hands to the roof, 'let's just say, the church accounts have not balanced once since *she* took over.'

Mercifully the sat nav announced that we had arrived at our destination.

We were shown to our room. A double bed with a single squeezed in at the side of it. At least I didn't have to sleep in the same bed, I hadn't done that since I was 3 and had peed mine. I'd climbed in next to her, snuggled up and shared my urine-soaked nighty with her.

Thereafter, I was banned outright from my mother's bed.

We had been booked in for a swim and then a facial. I hated swimming. For a Pisces, I was a pathetic swimmer. Even worse, I hated swimming with kids. Especially the after-swim bit.

It was an unspoken rule that a parent had to stand, dripping and shivering while they dried and dressed their little Mer people. Then, by way of a thank you, they opened the changing room door just when your bare arse was gleaming to the room. I sighed, at least this time, my arse wouldn't be on display.

Looking down, I checked for spider's legs. All clear. I sucked in my gut and walked like a champion speed walker towards the pool area.

'No running.' Mr Tantastic in speedo's wagged a finger in my direction.

'I wasn't running, I was just trying to get into the…'

'Don't argue darling. Let's just enjoy our swim,' mum sashayed past me in a cloud of Coco Chanel, giving tan-man the eye.

For Christ's sake. Since the divorce, mum ran hot and cold. One minute she hated all men, the next, she was flirting like a horny teenager and didn't care how old [or young] they were.

Awesome. Today was a horny teenager day.

We swam, she chatted, I gasped for air and tried to keep my chin out of the water. I looked like Bruce Forsyth's love child. Chin-chin.

The facial was more relaxing, mainly because mum had opted for the face-wrap which mean she couldn't talk. I lifted one cucumber slice and looked at her, only her nose protruded from the wrapping, like an incomplete Halloween mummy.

I wished that I'd picked up my phone, it was blackmail material that Margaret Fucking Thompson would have paid handsomely for.

Back in the room, I laid on the single bed and revelled in the peace. Mum had gone to raid the onsite designer products shop. I couldn't afford luxury anything, never mind the layers of face creams that came with a heftier price tag than my mortgage payment.

My phone notified me that I had a message. The coven, checking to see if I'd strangled her yet.

I laughed and replied, *"Not yet, going to try the laxatives first, bahahahaha."*

Messages from the dating site had gone unread. I clicked on them.

Carlos, 55. Spanish bullfighter.
'Hola hermosa' *[Hi beautiful]*
'Cabrearse' *[Piss-off, or thereabouts]* Carlos Bullshit-os.

John, 51. Product manager.

John liked skiing and romantic log cabin breaks. He looked ok. I read his message.

On my profile, I'd put that I not only had kids, but I also had dogs.

John's message wasn't a hello. John's message was a bloody huge rant about how no one should have and domesticate a dog. They were wild animals, and anyone who thought that they had a god given right to domesticate a wild animal was a psychotic bastard exercising human dominance over nature etc etc.

I sighed. Oh John, you need to get out more.
I blocked the anti-domesticating knob-sack.

There was a message from Wilson. I had to read it twice. *"Got the dog again on Sunday if you fancy practising your gymnastic prowess?"*

I ignored the piss-take. So, the rat on a lead wasn't his then. Had he just asked me out for a dog walk?

I replied, *"Spa weekend with the mothership. Mud bath by intention this time."*

He replied with a Gif of a woman covered in tar, her gob wide open waiting for the cucumber slice to fall in it. Nice.

I must have fallen asleep because my mother did the 'not so subtle' cough as she stood over me.

'Fuck. Sorry. What time is it?' I yawned at her.

'For god's sake, don't swear. You sound so common. It's 5 o'clock. Dinner is at 7, I thought you would need the time to…' she waggled her hand in my general direction, 'sort yourself out.'

Two hours…. I could do it in ten minutes, mother dear.

She hadn't said anything as I'd emerged like a colourful butterfly from the bathroom. At least she hadn't criticised, I took that as a win.

After ordering a bottle from the bottom of the wine list, where the prices rise enormously, she seemed to relax as the server poured. Dinner was tiny. I wasn't expecting a Beano style slap-up meal, but the two cubes of paneer looked lonely in the pool of turmeric coloured gloop on my plate. Good job I'd stashed some crisps in my suitcase.

Another bottle of wine appeared. 'We didn't order that,' mum told the server.

'Madame, it is from the gentleman over there.' He indicated a dapper looking older chap sat a couple of tables away.

'Ah, of course, thank you,' Mum said it like she was expecting the wine. She waved like the Queen of Sheba in dapper chaps' general direction and smiled, whilst muttering at me 'Say thank you darling, don't be ignorant.'

I did a thumbs up, nodded and stabbed the last cube of paneer.

I noticed that my mum had changed her body language. Her knees were now directed more towards our anonymous wine donor. I was surprised that she hadn't asked to swap tables so that she could get a better view.

After dinner we relocated to the lounge, where candles had been lit and a bored and poorly paid pianist gently played.

As we sat, mum leaned into me, 'If he comes over, let me do the talking, and for fuck's sake, don't swear darling.'

How she missed the irony in that sentence was beyond me.

Mr Wine did indeed head our way, with a younger version of himself in tow. I hadn't noticed his youthful doppelganger at dinner and wondered how I'd missed him.

I heard mum's 'ooooh' and chose to ignore it.

I was astonished watching mum. She was probably the best flirter I had ever seen in action, even better than my non-related sister. With ease, she listened, added to the conversation, showing that she was both attentive and fascinating at the same time. She was indeed a fascinating woman but until now, I'd never seen her in full 'reel 'em in mode'.

The younger version had returned from his 'fresh air break'. He was a smoker and wafted his cigarette breath in my direction as he sat. He was also a valuer in the antiquities business and had travelled to places that I could only dream of. Lucky bastard.

He was 42, no children and really funny. His blue eyes sparkled when he laughed. Sitting there, watching mum enjoying herself and listening to Michael [as I now knew he was called] made such a pleasant end to the evening.

The bartender politely came over and declared that it was closing time and asked if we could finish our drinks. No landlady yelling 'time' here as she ushered the pissed up and paralytic away from the booze. This was a classy bar.

Mum and 'Roger' arranged a rendezvous after breakfast the next day, she looked expectantly at me and Michael. Sure, we'd hang out while our parents hooked up.

Air kisses were offered and received. Mum received an additional hand kiss and like a regal icon, she gracefully accepted.

Back in the room, mum flopped on her bed looking like a teen after their first date, all starry eyed and content.

'Roger, Roger, Roger. Yes please!' she laughed, a great, dirty, long laugh that certainly belonged to no teenager I'd ever met.

'What about you? Michael is gorgeous darling; you and he could be a thing! Imagine that! Double dating.' She looked at me eagerly as I pulled on my pyjamas.

I agreed that he was indeed very lovely, and I'd enjoyed his company and was looking forward to seeing him in the morning.

'Perfect. Of course, you'd need to make more of an effort. You wouldn't keep a man like Michael,' the hand waggled, 'wandering round in your scruffs.'

'Michael's gay mum.'

Her face fell an inch or two. 'Oh. Well, never mind. You can keep him company while Roger and I get to know each other better.'

Again, with the Sid James laugh.

It was going to be an interesting weekend.

Date 10 [or not]

She got us up at the crack of dawn to 'prepare' for yoga at 6am. I was NOT a yoga person. Having someone's arse crack 6 inches from my mat as they did the balasana pose, was not my idea of fun. I also had literally no balance.

Whilst mum managed the one-legged mountain pose, I toppled over. The instructor pointed to the bar at the side, 'For beginners,' he whispered, 'Go!'

Dismissed to the side of the room. I picked my nails and took a very long time tying my laces. Eventually, he rang the little bell and class was dismissed. Thank fuck.

'That was wonderful! I feel so invigorated,' mum declared as we made our way back to the room.

The way she had said 'invigorated' made me feel sorry for Roger, he had no idea what was coming.

I thought my teenage daughter took a long time in the bathroom but Christ, my mum took the biscuit. I was dying for a pee by the time she emerged. Steam worthy of a sauna explosion escaped from the bathroom behind her, like hands trying to pull her back in. Not a chance you steamy tendrils, I need the loo.

She had totally bombed the place. Discarded underwear, products from various expensive places I'd never visited, were strewn everywhere.

No! I was not *her* mum, I wasn't cleaning up after her. I left it all where it was.

Morning ablutions complete, I got changed.

She wandered back into the bathroom, 'Bloody hell Freya! You could have tidied up after yourself. Looks like a bloody bombsite in here'.

Words failed me.

We met Roger and Michael in the foyer. My mum, looking like Jane Fonda, greeted Roger like she had known him for years, 'Roger darling, so lovely to see you again.'

'Eloise, you look ravishing,' he charmed back.

Mum blushed like a coy Victorian spinster, although it was hard to tell under the amount of rouge she'd got on.

Apparently, our parents had arranged a round of golf. Golf, in my insignificant opinion, was one of the most tedious games ever invented. That was probably because I was utterly shite at it. I was left-handed with no coordination and doomed to be crap at ball games. Well, most of them anyway….

Michael, it turned out, was not a golfer either. After a few embarrassing swings and indiscreet sniggers from Roger and my mum, I retired to the sidelines.

Michael joined me, 'Come on, let's go and have brunch and leave them to it.' He paused and added, 'does she do this often?'

'What? Hook up with random strangers and take the piss out of her daughter. Yep.'

Roger apparently, did the same. They were made for each other.

Over brunch, it seemed that Michael was looking for more than just a casual hook-up. We discussed the perils of online dating, and I told him about a few of my disasters. To say he was amused was an understatement. He positively cried laughing. He shared his dating calamities, which to be fair, were quite similar to mine. It didn't seem to matter who you were looking for, there were a lot of dickheads to sift through.

We ogled the same arse, as a pair of tight black jeans walked past us.

'That one is mine!' he told me.

'No way, that's mine!' I laughed.

The guy turned around and smiled directly….. at Michael.

Typical. I sat there and finished my squished avocado on sour dough delight, while Michael made googly eyes with black jeans guy.

Even my mother could get a date. I secretly sulked. It all felt very unfair.

Michael and black jeans wandered off for a walk and left me to entertain myself. Even the server pissed off out of the room. Feeling somewhat leprous, I ambled away trying to smile, like I was happy be on my own.

Head held high in a haughty fuck you, I went out into the gardens and found a lonely bench. As a kindred soul, I felt it called to me.

I'd missed a call from Sarah. She'd also sent a text, *"Call me. Nothing to worry about."*

To a parent, that meant one thing. Panic. Had something happened with one of the kids?

One call back later, it seemed that Cal had possibly broken his collar bone playing his match and was on his way to A&E for an x-ray.

Fuck. I rang my mum as I charged back up to the room. I told her what had happened and that we had to leave. I may not always like my children but when they are hurt, they're the most precious thing on earth.

'Oh. Well, if you need to go, then go. I will just get in the way. Don't worry about me, I can get an Uber.'

I knew that she'd said that in the hope that Roger the dodger would take her home.

Whatever. It's only your grandson.

I must have driven like Lewis Hamilton [breaking no speed limits though, officer] and arrived at the hospital and speed walked like an Olympian through the corridor to find my boy.

'I'm ok mum,' Cal's pale face told me otherwise. I hugged Sarah, who explained events leading up to my son's downfall.

'Have they given you anything for the pain?'

He shook his head.

I found a nurse who gave my injured off-spring some pain medication. She told me that the doctor was on his way, so we shouldn't be waiting much longer.

The [incredibly dishy] doctor eventually arrived. Exchanging a few pleasantries with him was very nice indeed, but he had a job to do.

He approached my pale and very fed-up boy. 'Nice break young man, do you want to see?'

He showed us my son's cracked clavicle on the computer screen. We all crowded round. I could smell the doctor's aftershave, which was almost as nice as he was.

I was impressed and once again, spoke my thoughts out loud 'Your bones are quite beautiful. You evidently get that from me!'

Everyone in the room looked at me for one astonished second. Oh my god.

'Anyway. We can't do very much with these. We'll pop a sling on you, you'll need to keep it on for 2 weeks and no sports for 6 weeks.' The doctor delivered the blow to my son's sporting career without batting an eye.

I went to comfort my crestfallen boy and managed to add to his pain by hugging the damaged side. He yelled.

'You'll need to be careful with the hugs.' The dishy doctor winced.

Once the sling was supporting the damage. I took the doctor to one side.

'Sorry, doctor, I just wondered if I could ask you a couple of questions?'

'Call me Rob, it's nice to meet you.'

I smiled back and explained about the tournament coming up, 'It's in 6 weeks, well, 5 weeks and 5 days to be exact, can he play. Please?'

'Ideally, we want 6 weeks rest, but a couple of days shouldn't hurt. He just needs to be careful. I'll give you my number, in case you need it,' he paused and looked at me, 'or if you fancy dinner maybe?'

I giggled then. I *actually* giggled, like a love-struck boy band fan.

Get a bloody grip woman, you're making a complete tit of yourself.

'That would be nice, thank you,' I managed to reply like a grown-up, at least.

Sarah, Cal and I walked back through the waiting room. Andy Gilmore, the shouty sports teacher came striding over.

'Mate, are you ok?'. He addressed my son, completely ignoring us.

Cal explained that he was off sports for 6 weeks. As big as he was now, his chin wobbled like it did when he was little.

Like a heroine, I delivered the news that would save the day. 'You can still play in the tournament; I asked Rob, you know, the dishy doctor, and he said you could play.'

I aimed for reassuring.

'Christ mum, I've broken a bone and you're trying to get a date.' He walked off.

Andy Gilmore just stared at me. Just stared. Sarah told him we would let him know how things were going and excused us.

There are times when I've made a complete arse of myself, usually in public, but this was far worse. I'd upset my son without intending to and made myself look like a succubus on the hunt.

I decided that it wouldn't be wise to go for dinner with Doctor Rob, I didn't think my boy would ever forgive me.

***

I settled my son into bed, made sure he had everything he needed to hand, the left hand. His right hand was encased in the sling.

Sarah had made me a consolatory coffee. 'He'll be fine. He'll heal quickly and the whole thing will all soon be forgotten. Don't worry about it.'

But I did worry. Had I become so obsessed with getting a date that I'd been eyeing up the doctor treating my son for a broken bone. I was a shitty mother and told her so.

'A shitty mother wouldn't have broken the sound barrier to get to her injured child, would she?! Quit with the self-pity, it doesn't suit you.'

Blimey, she could be all headmistress when she wanted to be.

My injured son was safely asleep by 10pm. I laid in bed and stared at the ceiling. My phone lit up. Wilson.

"How's he doing? Hope he's ok. My youngest broke her collar bone last year. They heal quickly. It's just a bit shit for them for a few weeks."

"Thanks. He's ok, asleep. Gutted about not training though." I added a teary face to emphasise the upset.

"Yeah. Andy said. So, did you get a date with the doc?" He added a laughing crying face.

Even Wilson thought I was a piranha.

"No. Not a priority."

Bugger off Wilson. I didn't need reminding of the world's view of my dating efforts. Shouty Gilmore must have bust a gut to tell him about my epic faux pas. I didn't appreciate that very much.

***

For the next few weeks, I focussed my energy on being the best mum/nurse/waitress/taxi service, a child could want. Dating could just fuck right off.

I carried the guilt I felt around like a millstone. Maybe I was just too long in the tooth for this dating malarky, it hadn't done much to make me feel good about myself so far.

In fact, all in had done was to make me feel really crap. It had knocked my confidence and smashed my hope. Hope and love are what make us human and right now, I didn't particularly feel loved, and as for hope. Dying embers there.

Maybe I should just concentrate on being the best mum and person that I could be and focus all my energy into that. I rang my non-related sister.

'Don't be such a defeatist! So what? You tripped up a few times, big deal. Anyway, you can't give up. I've booked us onto something exciting!' She slapped me down and presented a teaser all in one very quick sentence.

Charlotte refused to give any more details other than the kids were all sorted for the weekend, and I had to be ready for 7.30pm on the following Friday.

Whilst I loved Charlotte, I did not love surprises. I'm a 'need to know what's happening' kind of person.

As a result, the week went very slowly in a sea of 'not telling you' texts and emojis.

ARGH!

Dates 11 – 19

Despite my best efforts, Charlotte gave nothing away. She'd simply told me *"Dress nice, see you at 7.30!"* on her last text.

Dress nice? What did that mean? Was a dress and heels nice? Jeans and a top? I decided that I wasn't going to wear a dress. I never felt as confident in a dress as I did in jeans. My dresses were the clingy type which meant that if whatever she'd planned involved eating, I was going to end up with a bloated toddler belly.

I went for nice black jeans and a halter top. It showed off the curves without whacking them in someone's face. Perfect for a walk into the unknown. Wedge sandals would be better than pointy demon heels.

One thing I always avoided in demon heels was a slippery floor. The slightest hint of a glossy sheen and I was over like a newborn giraffe on an ice rink, accompanied by a sudden seagull shriek.

I stared at my face for a while in the mirror. It was a lived in face but not neglected. It was more of a tired t-shirt face. Faded a bit but you could still see it had a few outings left in it and I'd always been told that I had a great smile and really nice eyes.

My nice eyes were ruined with poorly judged mascara wand that caused watery eye syndrome, and I had to start my make-up again. The hair decided it was going to have a good day, at least I could hide the eye-puff behind my long fringe.

The lure of a takeaway and Sky Cinema was all it had taken for the kids to skip happily away after Rachel, the Pied Piper of babysitting.

With no one to grunt approval at my transformation, I walked out to the taxi.

Charlotte took one look at me, "Perfect! You look ace! And don't ask me where we're going, you'll find out when we get there.'

I complimented her, she always looked disgustingly stunning. She had the unusual natural combination of very dark hair and piercing blue eyes. Compliments exchanged, off we went, into the unknown.

The taxi pulled up outside of a huge hotel, one of those that looks like rabbit hutches had been stacked up on top of each other. Still none the wiser, I followed her in.

And then I saw it. The sign. A goddamned huge sign pointing to the conference room.

Speed Dating Night 1

'Oh my god. No!'

'Oh my god, yes! It's going to be so much fun.' She grabbed my hand and dragged me through the swathes of beige furnishings.

'I thought you were off dating,' I protested.

'I was, but you live and learn. I've lived and I've learnt. No more dickheads for me. Let's go!'

A woman greeted us through such a thick layer of make-up that she reminded me of the Boots counter assistants in the 90's.

We were given a sheet of rules to read before signing our agreement to the evening.

Rules.
1. Respect personal boundaries
2. Follow your host's instructions
3. Treat everyone with respect
4. Keep an open mind
5. Maintain a balanced conversation
6. Have fun

The rules seemed sensible; I should've had applied them to my previous dates.

There was a 5-minute slot for each 'date'. At the end of the 5 minutes, a buzzer would sound. The next person then arrived for their chance to impress you, and you them.

Each hopeful woman would be sat at one side of the table in a 3-sided booth.

A chap would sit opposite, and the game would begin.

A bit like a job interview, apparently you circled yes or no on your pad. A yes meant a possible match, a no meant, well, no.

Looking around the room, all I could see were women. The gorgeous, the glamourous and the gifted game hunters.

'Where are the men?' I whispered.

'They come in after we are seated so there's no cheating, they've pre-selected some of them.' she beamed.

The hostess with the mostest [make-up] gave us all a number and directed us to the drinks. God, I needed a drink. I'd been given number 17. My lucky number. Maybe this was going to be worthwhile after all.

Nervous [me] excited [her], we guzzled our drinks, then grabbed another.

I was directed to a booth and plonked my number on the table. I waved across the room at Charlotte, who waved back enthusiastically.

Like a power mad teacher on exam day, the hostess told us all to be seated. The doors opened and the potential suitors filed in.

Holy fuck, it was intense.

What was I going to say? By the time I'd stammered hello, I was sure that my 5 minutes would be up. I could imagine all the circled 'No's' on their pads for number 17, the bumbling buffoon.

I could see guys had started sitting at the booths across the room. Victim number 1, or number 24 as he turned out to be, arrived at my booth. He very carefully placed his number card on the table and held out his hand.

Formally, we shook slightly sweaty hands.

Number 24 was Simon. An electrician. I introduced myself, and for some reason I then blurted 'I'm divorced with children and dogs. I think I'm considered middle aged and I'm tall with heels on. Hope none of that is a problem.'

All the things that had been issues in my dates came tumbling out at once, like a stream of sewage from a broken pipe.

Simon looked from side to side, like a response to my statements could be found there.

'Erm, ok.'

'Sorry, I'm just nervous. Never done this before. Well, I *have* dated obviously, been married a few times, so duh. What I mean is, I've not been speed dating before, so not really sure what the protocol is.' I finally drew a breath.

Simon smiled politely, picked up his pad and blatantly circled NO. He stood up ready to move on before the buzzer had even sounded.

Awesome start.

I could see Charlotte looking past her hopeful date, towards me. I just shrugged. What else could I do?

Smile apparently. She did the smile mime and followed it with a Wallace and Gromit grin.

Smile. Yes.

Number 25 arrived, another Jason. Lovely smile and he asked how I was.

'In all honesty, this is stressful as hell.' I told him.

He agreed but said it would get better, he'd been doing these for a few months now and although he'd never clicked with anyone, he was ever hopeful.

Whilst Jason was not physically my type, he was a nice guy to have a quick chat to and helped me to relax, for which I thanked him. I couldn't see whether he circled yes or no but I felt a bit of a shit circling 'No'. He was very sweet.

Number 26 quickly arrived, like he had no time to waste.

Brian, it seemed had a lot of allergies. Not only did Brian spend the first 30 seconds with a Vicks nasal spray rammed up his right nostril, but he constantly snorted. The back of the throat glob of goo type dirty pig of a snort.

He finished his five minutes by gobbing a loogie into a hanky, folded that soggy cotton square and stuffed it into his brown trousers pocket.

As I circled 'No', I wondered where the hand sanitiser was.

Number 27 stepped around the booth. Standing in front of me was none other than Wilson.

Fuck, fuck, fuck. My mouth fell open like a baby bird waiting for a half-chewed caterpillar. There was nowhere to hide. I felt my face burn and knew my neck had gone blotchy.

He laughed, 'Hey. I didn't know you were gonna be here. How's it gone so far?'

'Oh lord.' I sighed.

'Zak is fine, no need to do the lord bit, I'm off duty.'

I laughed. 'Arse'.

I can honestly say it was the most relaxed 5-minutes that I'd spent with anyone in ages. Wilson had also been dragged along by a friend and had zero expectations.

I declared that, so far, present company excluded, it was a 5-minute shit-fest but the wine was decent.

The buzzer sounded and made me jump.

And just like that, number 27 moved along the conveyor belt of speed dating.

My pen hovered, he was a million years younger than me, so it was going to have to be a no, but circling 'No' would be mean. Like me, he couldn't help his age, I just couldn't circle 'No'.

I left it blank.

Number 28 rounded the corner and was quite frankly, a huge disappointment in comparison to his predecessor.

Martin didn't have a lot to say other than, 'I don't think any of this is for me.'

He looked like he was about to cry.

I tried to calm him and told him to enjoy it, and that there was someone for everyone. By the time the buzzer sounded, I felt like I'd been speaking to one of my twins after another [short-lived] heartbreak.

Before **number 29** arrived, I tried to chug the last of my wine. Mistake. I choked, not because of the wine but because number 29 was Andy Gilmore, the shouty knobhead of a sports teacher.

'Oh. Hi,' he managed to sound disappointed as he sat down.

As usual, my gob opened before my social filter had engaged, 'Oh. You. I was hoping for vegetable rice.'

'What?'

Jesus, what had I just said? I mentally facepalmed.

'Sorry, no. I mean. Number 29 at the local Chinese is vegetable rice.'

He brushed his long fringe out of his eyes, 'No, it's just me, minus vegetables… or rice. How's the dating going? Not well I'm guessing as you're sat here.'

Oh Sherlock, your incredible powers of observation simply astound me.

'It's like swimming through treacle, only not as tasty.'

'Rots your teeth. Treacle I mean, not swimming.'

Was he saying I had terrible teeth?

'So, you're the friend that Wilson came with?'

The conversation was fading quicker than my enthusiasm for the evening.

'Yeah. We thought it might have been fun.' Past tense.

It isn't fun Andy because I'm here trying to make small talk with you and avoiding any further mention of food.

He asked me how my son was and sympathised at his frustration. Andy assured me that he would be ok for the tournament.

He actually smiled then, and for the first time I noticed he had dimples and smattering of freckles. Cute.

I've always loved freckles and have never understood why people cover them with make-up. They're beautiful.

The buzzer brought me back to reality.

'Well, it's been nice talking to you. Apologies for the lack of food. See you soon.' With that he moved along to the next booth.

I looked up and saw that Wilson had reached my non-related sister.

She was sat with her seductive smile and head tilt, Charlotte only saved that for disarming and charming.

Interesting.

Numbers 30, 31 and 32 might have been triplets. All three of them looked almost identical. Clothing and hair styled like a 3 for the price of 2.

In the monotone voices of children in their nativity, they asked the same generic things. I wondered if they'd scripted their imaginative questions together in the pub round the corner.

- What do you do for a living?
- What are your hobbies?
- What are your favourite films?

Number 32 also added a conversation stopper.

- Do you like rubber knickers?

What the fuck? Had I heard that right? Rubber knickers? Urgh. Why would anyone want that kind of sweat-fest around their bits?

Huge circle round the 'NO' for number 32.

With the so-called speedy bit of the dating over. We had to hand in our notepads. Apart from the blank 2, mine were all intense 'No's', and I'd only left the other 2 blank because I'd have felt shitty circling no.

'What happens now?' I asked Charlotte who was grinning like a kid given a tenner in a sweet shop.

'Ha, that's the best bit about this. They go through our answers and tomorrow night, they arrange a meet for those who have matched.'

'What? There's another evening of this?' I stared at her.

'Oh yeah!' Charlotte danced on the spot.

'But….I've said no to everyone! I won't have a match for tomorrow.'

'Well, it's still possible if someone has said yes and they think you match, *but* only if they think you match.' She reassured me.

Shit, I hoped not. It would be like school rounders teams all over again. Added by the teacher to a resentful team who lobbed the left-handed, crappy catcher on 2nd post fielder, where no one ever hit the ball.

Great.

Dates 20 – 23

I laid in bed and replayed the evenings' events. I had, again, probably made a superb tit of myself. Besides the fact that I'd said no to everyone, with all the bumbling, blurting and waffling I'd done, I knew I wouldn't have a match

I then went into panic mode, but what if rubber knickers had circled a yes and the hostess had decided we were a perfect match. Holy fuck.

When I finally fell asleep, my dreams were haunted by a walking Vicks inhaler in sweaty rubber pants snorting its way towards me. I slept worse than a toddler with chicken pox.

The next morning, the eyebags sat there like two suitcases in lost luggage. Awesome.

My phone rang, 'Check you emails! I've forwarded yours.'

Apparently, the team behind speed dating hell emailed to say whether you have matches and only then, they gave out the details of where that evenings' meet would be. What they don't tell you is who you've been matched with.

'Before I open this, I need to check that I've understood it.' I paused, 'So, I could still be matched with the clone triplets even though I'd circled no, but *only* if they've circled yes and Madam Make-up decides we're a match?' I already knew the answer but was delaying opening the email.

'Yeah, I told you. That's why this one is so good! Normally only the matching yes's get through, but the idea is that we work through first impressions,' she cackled.

'If I've got Mr rubber knickers, I'm not fucking going, you know that right?' I was being firm.

The cackle again, 'Freya, if you've got a match, even if it *is* rubber knickers, you're going! Just think of the free wine!'

The cackling hag rang off and I opened the email with one eye closed.

Why I did that, I never knew. It made no difference to what was there. It was like something left over from childhood, don't look and the bogey man isn't really there….. just as he rips your arm off.

I stared at the screen. Holy crap. I'd been matched with 4 people. How the fuck had that happened? I'd said no to everyone but Wilson and Shouty, and I'd left them blank. I trawled through the memories of the previous night, not one of them stood out as anyone I'd like to spend more time with. Well, apart from Wilson but he was not relationship material, he was just turning out to be a nice guy.

A text from Charlotte came through, *"How many matches did you get?"*

Feeling like I'd been swindled, hoodwinked and bloody duped, I replied. *"Four."* Sad face emoji.

"Stop sulking you miserable cow. Four is ace!!" Happy face, party face emoji. *"I got 4 too. Pick me up just before 7, we'll have a quick drink first."*

Oh, what the hell, the least I could do was play love assistant to Charlotte the harlot on her quest.

I replied, *'Fine. You owe me!'*

I couldn't wear the previous night's clothes, so I spend the next 2 hours lobbing clothes around like a kid looking for their PE shorts on a Monday morning.

Eventually, I settled on a jumpsuit. It was a gamble. Jumpsuits are great BUT you have to strip off to have a pee, and if they're cheaply made, you're in danger of having the camel toe from hell.

I checked my messages on the dating site, nothing. I wasn't sure whether to be insulted or relieved by the big fat nothing.

I'd got a text from my daughter. No words, no hello, just a link to something else she wanted from Amazon. That was her usual form of communication. At least I knew she was ok, a kidnapper would hardly send me a link for curling tongs, would they?

The taxi arrived 5 minutes early, I gave each dog a treat as I left whilst carefully avoiding collecting dog hairs. The dogs understood that a treat meant abandonment for a few hours. They cared about the treat, not the abandonment.

It worked for the kids too.

***

A different venue awaited us, but we headed to the pub around the corner first. Regretting my decision to wear a jumpsuit, I tried to discreetly pull the crotch from my nethers' as I walked. I just looked like I'd got worms.

As we sat down our conversation inevitably turned to the matches.

'Who do you think you've got?' I asked.

She shrugged, 'Don't know, but I hope that teacher of yours is one of them!'

Charlotte's dirty laugh filled the bar.

Wilson would be perfect for her.

'I hope I haven't got Carl, the one with the thingy,' she wiggled her fingers at her face.

I laughed, 'Beard.'

Carl had a beard that would have made Hagrid jealous. We'd both noticed the egg [or at least I hope it was egg] stuck in it. It wiggled as he'd talked, like it was reaching out and trying to jump ship.

I hadn't had Carl as a match but had chatted to him at the bar. I'd quite liked his conversation, but I had found myself talking to his beard stowaway, rather than to him.

'Who do you think you've got?' She asked.

'No idea, but I'm telling you now, if its rubber knickers, I'm refusing, end of!' I wasn't going to sit anywhere near him again, 'Oh, bloody hell, please don't let it be Brian either.' I shuddered at the thought.

We got to the venue and were ushered to the bar. Good start, but I needed to slow down on the vino if I had any chance of holding a conversation without slurring.

With less make-up on, the hostess came round and gave us all an envelope. Inside were the numbers that we'd been matched with. I stared at mine.

'Ooooooh, look,' Charlotte held her card up to me, 'Get in! The teacher AND the arty guy. Hmm, number 26 and, who was number 23?'

I shrugged. I didn't remember a 23.

'Who've you got?' She snatched my card and laughed, '24, 26, teacher boy and 29. Oooh, this is going to be fun!'

Not really. Why I'd been matched with Wilson was beyond me. Jesus, 26 was fucking Brian, he of the Vicks nightmare.

'Oh no, 24 is my bumbling opener. I clearly saw him put a no. Why have I got him?' I sighed. Great, I'd also got vegetable rice.

The hostess told us that this time we had 20 minutes with each match. After which, we decided on one, and then had the chance to spend the remaining hour with just them.

It felt cruel. You were expected to reject someone who was in the same room. Rejected souls would then be ushered through to the other bar where there was a buffet laid out as a consolation prize. There, the spurned and unwanted could stuff their faces.

I had the wrong outfit on to be a face stuffer. Please, please don't let me be sent to the reject room. Then, I realised that both me *and* the person I had been matched with would have to say yes to spending the final hour in each other's company. Looking at the limp card in my hand, I knew I was heading to the reject room.

So instead, I muttered a prayer to the deity of dating, 'I'm going to the reject room, but please don't let me be the first one in there.'

This time there were a dozen tables set out in the room. Each woman had to approach their match. Bollocks, that meant no more wine for me. I was already feeling a little unsteady on the heels. Even Michelle Pfeiffer would look like a pantomime dame drunkenly weaving across a room.

And so, it began.

I wandered over to Simon and his big **number 24** lopsidedly sitting in the little stand.

'Erm. Hi. I'm not sure how we got paired and I'm sorry that I was a rambling nightmare last night.' I went for humble and apologetic from the off.

'Not sure either. I put you down as a 'No', I'm guessing you did the same. Maybe they're just filling places.' He was very nice about it.

With the pressure off we just had a nice, relaxed chat. Simon had started his own business as an electrician and told me a few tales of terrible customers hoping his re-wiring prowess was going to be a bit more personal. I told him about my job and a few pitfalls of managing a very young team. I had no idea what half of their words meant, 'yoof' was a very strange language.

The buzzer went and I'd genuinely enjoyed the chat. More than that, I felt a bit less wobbly. We both agreed that it was a no though, nice as the chat was, we were not destined to do the outstretched arms on the Titanic bit together.

I heard **number 26**, Brian before I saw him.

Fucking sniff, snort, sniff.

OMG, how was I going to get through 20 minutes with that noise rattling against my eardrums?

'Hey babe, glad we matched.' Brian clearly decided that was the moment to hack up phlegm, chew it a bit and swallow it down. He then started nibbling on the cold sore that had sprung up on his bottom lip.

That was a record. He'd managed to make me feel physically sick and to want to hit him in under 4 seconds.

I hated being called babe, I'm not a talking pig.

I took a deep breath, 'With respect Brian,' I used that line at work a lot. Usually when higher level management were trying to implement changes, and they hadn't got a sodding clue about how things actually operate, 'I think there has been a mistake, I'm afraid I circled no.'

I waited for the penny to drop. Nothing. No acknowledgement at all that I had basically just remined him that I'd rejected him less than 24 hours previously. And was now, rejecting him all over again.

He continued to snort and hock up phlegm to chew on. Four minutes and 10 seconds in, I could take no more. I excused myself and headed to the bathroom.

***

A sobbing woman shuffled into the toilets, her ponytail so high and tight, it made her look permanently surprised. She was immediately followed by a concerned friend. At least someone else was evidently having the same awesome time that I was.

Dabbing rivers of mascara, she let it out, 'What a prick! He just told me that he wasn't here for me, he was here for one of his other matches. I can't believe it, I thought we had a future!'

A future? You met the guy for 5 minutes yesterday.

'I told him I loved his freckles, and our children would be beautiful'. The friend just looked at me blankly and mouthed, 'Oh god.

Yep, I'm afraid your mate is a bunny boiler.

I timed it beautifully, as I arrived back at Brian's table the buzzer went. I bade him farewell [forever] and I wandered over to Wilson's table.

'Hello! Not sure how we got matched but at least it's a reprieve from the ass-wipes.' As always, my opening line was a stunner.

He smiled, 'Well, I said yes, what did you put?'

My face on fire, I replied honestly. 'I left it blank. I couldn't put no because you're, well, you're nice, but I couldn't put yes because.'

How could I say it?

He leaned forward, obviously enjoying my squirming, 'Because?'

'Well, you're, you know, a teacher. My kids' teacher and more than that, you're like, a third of my age.'

Very articulate.

He shrugged. 'Age doesn't count for diddly shit and as for being a teacher, we are allowed to have relationships with other grown-ups you know. We teach sex-ed in school, so I'm up on the latest info too.'

Oh fuck.

'It's fine, relax, I'm just jesting. I'm glad we've got the chance to have a chat though, I was going to ask you about your friend.' He indicated across the room.

All became clear.

Relieved, I smiled, 'Okay. What about her? You got a match with her too, haven't you? I'm thinking that's an intentional one!'

He asked a few questions about her, which I answered as honestly as I could.

The buzzer sounded and it was time to move on.

'Enjoy!' I told him.

'You too, you've got Andy next, haven't you?'

I nodded, 'Yeah. Hopefully he'll be using his inside voice today!'.

He turned serious, 'Give him a chance Freya, he's a really good guy and he likes you.' He smiled then, 'God knows why, but he does.'

Before I could register what he'd just said, my non-related sister was standing next to me, 'Bugger off then woman!'

I tottered along to the next table where Andy was sat looking a bit puzzled.

'You weren't expecting me?' I hoped this wasn't about to be another humiliating shit show.

'I certainly was,' he smiled, 'Be seated, oh great one.'

I ignored that. 'How's it going?'

He grimaced and told me that he thought he'd upset someone [again] and apparently, she'd thought a match meant they were destined for all eternity. I watched him chatting freely and was once again drawn to his freckles…..

'Freckles!' I declared.

'Freckles? What?'

'The woman with the ponytail in the bathroom! That's who you upset! She was sobbing about a guy who she really liked and said your children would be beautiful!'

He groaned. 'Yeah, that sounds like her. Oh god, was she telling everyone?'

'About your freckles or the fact that she was having your babies after a 5-minute speed date?' I laughed, 'Don't worry, we've all had crap dates!'

I told him about the date I had as a teenager. The guy took a packet of baby wipes when we went bowling. I thought he had a bit of a clean hands' thing, which would have been fair enough, but no. He tried to clean my face with them before he came in for a snog. Thus rang the death knoll of that teenage romance.

He shared a similar emotionally scarring experience about the time he'd gone to kiss a girl outside of the youth club.

'She just latched on like Pacman. I ran all the way home and cried on my mum.' He admitted.

'Jesus! Poor 10-year-old you!' The vision of a little freckle faced Andy running home to his mum after being half eaten alive, was so funny, and sweet.

Suddenly, the buzzer sounded, and it was decision time. I left Andy to it without discussing our immediate future.

I was struggling with the jumpsuit as I stood. Everyone handed in their cards. I headed to the bar, ordered a couple of drinks and waited for Charlotte to join me, while the points were scored and the walks of shame to the buffet were announced.

Charlotte flounced over smiling. 'I've *really* enjoyed this so far, cheers!' Her glass rang against mine as the hostess made her way through the room.

Waving their cards, she adopted her pity face as she approached Bogey Brian and Bunny Boiler, who wandered off towards the gates of reject city together.

The wine was very welcome as we awaited our fate.

Date 24

I couldn't see Wilson or Andy in the room. Had they said no to everyone and left?

'Do you think you've got a final date?' I asked. I was getting really nervous about joining the plates of sausage rolls and soggy sarnies, especially as Brian was already in there.

She grinned, 'Yep, I think I might have.,' she nodded towards the exit, 'At least snotbox has gone.'

'Fuckin' hell, that man drove me insane, I took a long bog break. Just couldn't handle,' I snorted and sniffed, 'anymore.'

'Me too. Told him I needed a crap.' She announced.

'Well, that's one way to do it!'

The hostess was getting nearer, and I found myself holding my breath. She tottered along the bar and looked like she had been helping herself to the free wine, '16 and 17?'

'Yep, that's us.' we confirmed.

She spun round, 'Ah, there you are. 16, you have a final date. He's on table 6. And…. 17. Oh, look at that, congratulations. Final date for you too. Table 4.'

She sounded surprised that I'd managed a final date, but not as surprised as I was. I'd expected to be ushered in shame towards the soggy vol-au-vents.

'Yus! See you on the other side!' My non-related sister walked away like a woman on a mission to save the earth.

Table 4. God, I couldn't even look. All I knew was that Brian was out of the snotty question. I took a deep breath, grabbed my wine and tried to look elegant as I discreetly pulled the jumpsuit out of my arse crack.

I walked past table 6 and smiled, Wilson. I could hear Charlotte's dirty laugh. She was happy, and about bloody time too.

So, who was table 4.

'Please be seated while I grab my baby wipes,' Andy Gilmore sat at table 4, smiling.

'Hello freckles, our babies will be beautiful.'

He laughed, 'Fuck off!' he indicated to the door, 'I think she's gone to the room of doom.'

'With Bogey Brian. They make a stunning couple, although their snot ridden children will never have a small furry animal.'

In the hour that followed, I learned that Andy had never been married but had been in two long term relationships. By comparison, I felt like a cross between Jennifer Lopez and Christie Brinkley, with the looks and finances of neither.

He shared custody of his 2 kids. There was a menagerie of animals, 2 dogs, a goat called Bob, 4 ducks and 5 chickens.

I told him about knob-dog and his exuberant sidekick. He'd already heard about knob-dog from Wilson and had sympathy. Apparently, he also had a spoon of a dog that, like my ex-husband, liked to chase anything that moved.

'So how come you ended up on the dating scene? Zak showed me your profile, have to say, the photo doesn't do you justice.' He waited, smiling.

Was that a compliment?

'Oh. That was nice of him!' I sighed, 'I don't know. I guess after the divorce, I wanted to focus on the kids and my career. I've achieved a lot on my own, but I got to a point in life where I just, well, wanted to connect with someone real and start a new life journey.'

God, this had turned deep.

'And you chose online dating?' He laughed again, 'Bloody hell, are there any 'real' people on those sites? The ones Zak got were crackers. He got more pictures of boobs and offers of sex than Aerosmith. Some of them were mums from school!'.

I told him about the plastic Penelope's at parents' evenings, 'He always looked so frightened!'

'Some of them are lovely but honestly, dating a student's parent is really frowned upon, virtually against the rules. Mind you, some of them weren't interested in dating.' He winked at me.

Ah. If dating a parent was frowned upon, then there was going to be little chance of this moving beyond the evening. I was surprised that my heart sank a little bit at that.

I snuck a peak over at Wilson's table, they were laughing and looked so relaxed. No parental dating dilemmas there.

'So, what about you? Did you not join any online dating sites, or have you just been watching over Wilson's shoulder?'

'Nah, it's not for me. Since my split, I've been concentrating on my kids and the work I do with the youth teams, besides, I prefer to meet people the old-fashioned way, you know, in person.' He shrugged, 'People say whatever they want on those things, they can invent a story that Tolkien would be envious of. Then there's the stalkers, firecrackers and the desperately seeking anyone brigade.'

Hmm, I wondered which brigade I'd been put in.

'In case you're wondering, you're in firecracker.'

Before I could comment on that, my phone vibrated on the table. Fearing another broken bone, I checked it. Missed call from the mothership. I was about to ignore it when she rang again, that usually meant something was wrong.

'Sorry, just got to get this.' Then to the phone. 'Mum, you ok?'

A loud but broken Darth Vader came over the phone.

'Just… let you know…. And I…. married.'

'What? Mum! Where are you? Are you ok?'

'Yes! All good…. Roger asked…… next week.'

And with that, she had gone. I sat for a moment and stared at my phone and tried to piece the conversation together.

'What the hell was that?' I asked myself.

'Sounded like she was married, getting married or Roger was,' Andy offered.

Fuck's sake mother. Of course, she had to do something to interrupt what was a nice evening.

'Sorry. My mothership is a force known only unto herself. She said she was okay though, right?'

'Sounded that way from here. Ring her back if you're worried.'

My phone pinged. Message from the mothership,

"Sorry. Bad signal. On the yacht. Was ringing to let you know Roger and I are getting married!!' Wedding bell emoji.

'What the actual fuck? She's getting married to Roger the Dodger apparently. She's on a yacht, so obvs poor signal.'

Andy just looked at me for a moment and I realised that I'd had that little conversation with myself whilst doing my mother's voice about the yacht.

'Would you do it again, get married I mean?' he asked.

'Christ no. Never again. Can't say I didn't try, again and again, but no, it's not for me. I can honestly say that it's all a lot of stress for a huge anti-climax. A bit like first time sex.'

What? Bollocks! I'd done it again. I smiled apologetically for the comment.

'Right. Noted. And moving on…. Our hour is almost up.' He looked at the clock on the wall.

That was not a good sign, if he was clock watching, then he was obviously as bored as a kid at a christening. Great.

He continued, 'So, what happens now?'

'I think they ring the bell and that's it, isn't it. I'm not sure we get a chance to have salmonella sandwiches that Bogey and Bunny have probably gobbed on.'

'No, I meant, what happens with…' he was interrupted by the buzzer and the clapping of the hostess' hands.

'That's it my lovely lovers in waiting! Congratulations on your final dates! I do hope you'll send me invitations to your weddings.' She laughed a little to forcefully and obviously thought she was far more amusing than she was.

A polite applause broke out in the room.

'Oh please. Thank you, thank you. Do go through to the buffet if you would like to, it all needs eating up or I'll be taking it home in a doggy bag.'

Again, with the over-the-top laugh.

I wasn't sure what I was supposed to do now, and neither was Andy judging by his awkward stance.

I'd already noticed that his eyes had more colours than the paint cards at B&Q, but it wasn't until we waited for the other two, that I realised how tall he was.

I came up to his shoulder, in my heels. I wondered why I'd never noticed before. It just hadn't registered.

We both looked over at Wilson and my non-related sister, neither had moved from their seat.

I looked at Andy, 'Ever get the feeling that you're surplus to requirements?'

'Yep. Like a 3rd nipple.' He seemed to be thinking out loud and quickly added, 'not that *I* have a 3rd nipple or have even seen one… unless you count Scaramanga but his was plasticine.'

I burst out laughing. That was exactly the kind of mind trail I would have verbalised.

Wilson and Charlotte had finally moved, mainly because the hostess had politely ushered them from their chairs.

'So, what now? Are we calling it a night or heading off somewhere else?' Blimey, she was eager, this friend of mine.

Wilson looked at his watch, 'Its quarter past 10, I'm gonna have to get back for the babysitter. Don't want to annoy her, she might double her fee for next time.'

We walked out slowly behind the two love birds. Andy and I had that awkward dangly arm thing. Neither of us wanting to look like we were trying to grab a hand. Andy stuck his hands in his pockets. I did the half body hug thing which just made me look like I had belly ache.

As we filed out of the door, Andy stood back to let me go through first and, I noted, put his hand on the bottom of my back.

Houston! We have [physical] contact!

The other two exchanged numbers. Andy and I looked like a pair of awkward kids. Were we meant to swap numbers? Did he even want mine? Did I want his?

A lingering hug was exchanged between Wilson and Charlotte, whilst Andy and I just, well, kind of smiled at each other. We said goodnight without needing to call Houston again.

In the taxi, my non-related love bird squealed, 'Oh my fucking god. He is beaut!', she let out the sigh of the freshly loved up.

As if she'd remembered I was there, she sat up, 'What about you? Are you and Andy Pandy gonna hook up? He is a total beaut too, not as much as Zak of course!'

I shrugged, 'Don't know. It was kind of awkward at the end. I felt a bit of a pillock.'

'Pah! Message him later!'

My confession that I hadn't got Andy's number didn't go down well.

'For fuck's sake woman. I'll sort it.' She declared as she decanted herself from the taxi.

Sort it? What if he didn't want to 'sort it' and swap numbers. The self-doubt hurled itself at me like a rugby player at the touchline.

Anyway, he'd said it was basically against the rules to date a parent, hadn't he?

I went to bed with mixed feelings.

The dogs joined me in my misery and decided that I only need 3 inches of bed and no duvet. The shits.

Date 25

I'd slept in. Knackered and a bit disorientated, I took the dogs out and battled with knob-dog when an off-lead chihuahua thought it would be a good idea to try to bite him.

I cursed the idiots who didn't keep their vicious squirrel under control, got home and headed for a shower.

Halfway up the stairs, I remembered mum's message. Shit. I tried to ring her back and got her posh telephone voice telling the caller to 'leave a message dharlink.'

I hung up and sent a text to Rachel, I'd collect the kids soon. She replied immediately, she was dropping them off later, they'd booked tickets to the cinema. Harmless for the recovering Cal, who still had a few days to go before he was free to throw himself around again. It looked like I had a free day then.

The dogs started barking, someone was at the door. Checking nothing unsightly was hanging out, I opened the door to Charlotte looking like she'd just stepped out of a salon.

'Bloody hell! Get dressed, we're going out for lunch! I'll make a fresh coffee,' she pushed past me and greeted the dogs like old friends on her way to the kitchen.

'Lunch? What about the kids?'

'They're sorted 'til teatime, aren't they? Shift, go and get your face on!'

'How do you know that the kids are sorted?'

'Rachel messaged me. Now move. Shower. Face.' She wasn't taking no for an answer.

'What am I wearing?'

'Well right now, your stinking dressing gown and those ugly grey pants. Get dressed! We're going to the Boathouse for lunch, I've booked a table. Thought we could go for a walk round there first.' She told me.

The Boathouse was in the middle of a forest. It had never been anywhere near a body of water. It was one of those odd historical things, no one knew why it was called the Boathouse. It just was.

Given that we were going for a walk, jeans and trainers were called for. I pulled my very faded but adored Kiss t-shirt on, tied my hair back, drank my coffee and offered the abandonment treats to the dogs.

She sang along to Pink as she drove. Pink was her go-to for getting in a party mood.

'Are we meeting anyone for lunch?' I had an odd feeling. Her pristine appearance, Pink and super hyped mood made my spidey senses shout.

'Can't I just be happy?' she laughed, 'Besides, if we were, would it be a problem?'

'Depends. If I'm going to be sitting there like a gooseberry while you and Wilson making moony eyes at each other, then yes!'

'Behave! You're not playing gooseberry.'

Half an hour later and we pulled up in the car park. Dogs weaved in and out of the trees waiting for their too-slow owners to catch up.

'Let's head up here.' And off she yomped, like a professional rambler, into the trees.

'You ok?' I'd caught up to her and could see the undisguised excitement on her face.

'I am better than ok, I'm perfect, apparently.'

Ahhhh, Wilson.

'Come on, spill! What's he said?' I couldn't help but smile at her. It was like she'd woken up from a really long kip.

She told me that they'd talked and messaged most of the night. I was a bit jealous; she'd hardly had any sleep and still looked that fresh. I was a sweating wreck; I could feel the under-boob drip making its way over my belly. I used my t-shirt to dry it off. Great, now I had two obvious wet patches that matched my underwire.

She hardly stopped talking to draw a breath. By the time we reached the Boathouse, I felt like I knew more about Wilson than I did any of my ex-husbands.

She floated in through the door. I panted inelegantly behind her. The server showed us to our table.

By the time I sat down, my hair was plastered to my neck. 'I'm gonna have to go and stick my head under the drier, back in a sec.'

I looked at myself in the mirror, with mascara smudged under both eyes, I could have passed for an elderly goth at a Sisters of Mercy gig.

Fucking great.

Ten minutes later, I gave up on drying the under-boob. At least my hair was dry, and I wandered back to our table.

Or at least what I'd thought was our table. A mop of dark hair was sitting there. Confused, I looked round. Had I lost a marble on the way to the bathroom?

Then I saw her, sat in the window seat… with Wilson.

Erm, ok. She waved and pointed to our former table and mouthed, 'You're there.'

'Eh?' I looked around.

The mare had set me up.

Andy Gilmore turned around, 'Oh, hello again. I guess this explains it. I think we've been set up.'

'Oh, have we! I thought I was having lunch with the *shittiest* friend in the world.' I emphasised the shittiest friend bit so she would hear.

'Well. You might as well sit down. I think they're gonna be a while, and you look like you need a drink, your kind of…' he pointed to the damp under-boob.

'Sweaty is the word you're looking for! She made me walk at 100 miles an hour; this is my exercise glow.'

'Suits you. We're here now might as well make the most of it. Nice t-shirt by the way.' He smiled. Andy seemed very relaxed with the fact that his shitty friend must have been in on this.

'I enjoy last night. Not the bunny boiler bit, I enjoyed the 'you' bit.' He announced.

Oooh. Nice to know.

Smiles all round for table 10.

'Yeah, it was good, in the end.' I smiled, ignoring the evil friend who I could hear laughing.

We ordered and waited for our drinks.

'So, I take it that you didn't know I was going to be here?' he was looking straight at me with the B&Q paint chart eyes.

'Nope. I thought I was having lunch with the snake over there!' I looked over at her, I don't think she was aware of anyone else in the room at that point.

'How do you feel about it being me instead of Polly Python?' he waited.

Be honest I told myself, 'You know, I'm really happy it's you. She's a shit friend anyway!'

We sat and chatted away like the date was intentional until our lunch arrived. I had a momentary panic then. I found it hard to eat in front of someone that I didn't know and holy crap, worse than that, what if he chewed like a camel?

Oh god, please don't let him be a chewy chewer.

Andy was NOT a noisy eater, even given that he might have been on his best chewing behaviour, he ate really nicely. Perfectly in fact!

My ex-husband had been a disgusting eater. Talking with his mouth full, like a washing machine, you could see the contents spinning around. Like a snake, he almost dislocated his jaw trying to ram too much in at once and then dropped food all over his face and top like a small child.

Andy was the complete opposite. Huzzah! I found that I could even eat in front of him without trying to hide my head under the table. Double Huzzah!

'Hi Andy! It's soooo nice to see you!' a voice purred from over my shoulder.

He looked up, 'Hi', he seemed to be struggling for a name, or reluctant to use it.

'It's Clare, Elliot's mum. You remember me of course!' She moved round to get a better look at me, her false eyelashes opened wider than shutters on a shop window, 'Oh, you're Cal's mum. Interesting.'

It was not said in a friendly way.

'Hi. Yeah, Freya... Cal's mum.'

She already knew that, the dipshit. I smiled falsely, 'How are you?'

Crap. Andy wasn't supposed to hang out with parents of students and Clare was not only a massive gossiping bitch, but she was also on the PTA [that I rarely attended]

'Oh, I'm *good*,' Clare emphasised the good and glanced at Andy again before continuing, 'Will Cal be playing in the tournament next week?'

She eyed me coldly.

'He should be good to, yeah, he's healed.' Fuck off Clare, you're not going to intimidate me.

'Great.' Said with no conviction, she then turned to Andy, 'It was nice to see *you*. Enjoy your lunch.' Clare walked away with a huge hair flick like she was in a shampoo commercial.

Andy looked at me, 'Well, that's given me indigestion.'

I laughed, 'Are you going to be hauled up to the head's office on Monday morning for hanging out with a parent?'

I saw Wilson watching over his shoulder.

Andy shook his head, 'No. I'll be fine.'

He said he'd be fine, but I'd noticed the tension in his shoulders. I sighed to myself; his shoulders were far nice to be tense.

Bloody hell. Behave.

Lunch hadn't ended on the high that I'd hoped for. Wilson and Charlotte paid their bill. Andy went to the bathroom, and rather than have an uncomfortable bill paying episode, I went and sorted ours.

I remembered the 'be pro-active' from the coven and took the opportunity to write my number on a scrap of paper and stuffed it in my pocket. If I wimped out and didn't give him my number, I knew I'd regret it.

He'd wandered back in and saw that I'd paid the bill, 'Oh, thanks. I owe you one.'

'I'll hold you to that.' As I said it, I resisted the urge to make some comment about holding *other* things, my mind however had no such resolve, and I smiled to myself.

Wilson and Andy had parked on the other side of the Boathouse, we all said our goodbyes in the car park. I didn't want another awkward parting, so I braved it, stepped up and gave Andy a hug.

Oh man, he smelt soooooo good.

He murmured in my ear, 'Thank you. It's been good to see you. Speak soon.'

As we stepped back, I shoved the crumpled paper into his hand. 'My number, in case you want it.'

'I do. Thanks.'

Yay, he'd said he wanted my number!

It was then that I noticed Clare leaving the Boathouse, she'd paused briefly, raised a perfectly plucked eyebrow and immediately reached for her phone. Bitch!

As we'd walked the long way round to get there, we followed the short-cut back to the car.

'Who was the hog with the hair? She seemed very interested in your Andy!' Charlotte obviously hadn't like Clare on sight. She had good taste.

'He isn't my Andy, you plum! Clare's one of the preened parents from school, her son plays in the team with Cal. The son is lovely, but she's an overindulged shit stirrer,' I paused, 'I hope she doesn't go causing problems for Andy. Did you know that it's frowned upon to date a parent?'

She shrugged, 'It's a conflict of interest isn't it.'

We said no more about the ethics of teachers dating parents. Instead, we took the piss out of Clare and her hair, and then sang very loudly to Pink all the way home.

I collected the kids and had a lovely catch up with Rachel's non-suffering husband, Ben. She was out at the gym.

When we arrived home, the kids disappeared into their rooms, and only came down for tea. As usual, they disappeared again before they had to fill the dishwasher.

Finn came over to me and hugged me, 'Mum, when I grow up, I want to be just like you and be the best dishwasher filler in the world.'

At least someone in the house recognised my skills.

Once he was safely tucked up in bed, I finally had time to think about the day. My phone pinged. Dating site message, shit, I'd forgotten about the dating site.

Somehow it felt wrong to be on a dating site now. Not that I was in any kind of *anything* with Andy, but being hooked up to it felt deceitful and I didn't know why.

Or did I?

Non-date 26

Monday had come around far too quickly, the usual mayhem of finding school shoes and bus passes filled the house.

I'd still had nothing from Andy, I wasn't sure what I'd been expecting, but I'd expected something at least.

Work went slowly. I had 2 complaints to deal with, both from the same whinging pillock. He'd moaned the previous month about our opening times. Fair enough. I'd asked him to put it in writing and said I'd send it up to the powers that be…who would look at it in 6 months and then throw it in the bin. This time however, he was complaining, at length, about the quality of the bog roll. He felt so strongly about it, that he'd sent it twice.

After 5 minutes of wishing he'd get to the point, the temptation to reply with 'Piss off Baldrick' almost got the better of me. Instead, I responded with a perfectly professional acknowledgement of his toilet roll concerns and a promise that it would be sent on.

Christ, some people had too much time on their hands.

My phone vibrated; my mum had sent a photo of my wedding invitation. They were getting married in the Maldives in 6 weeks' time.

Of course they were. She knew that I couldn't afford to go, and she knew the kids wouldn't be granted time off school.

A member of my staff team stood in the door to my office, 'Have you got a minute?', his youthful face was stern.

'Sure, come in. What's up?'.

His major concern was that he'd had to empty the office paper bin; it was full. He'd checked his contract, and it didn't state that bin emptying duty was part of his role.

I looked around, thinking that this was some kind of YouTube wind up. Was he actually fucking serious?

There are people dying in the world from disease and war, and this spoilt little mouse was kicking off because he had to empty a waste-paper basket.

Breath. Just breath.

'Jordan, in the big scheme of things, you know like war, poverty and climate change, emptying one waste bin is not going to kill you. If it's full, please just empty it.'

He was adamant, 'I've checked my contract, and it says nothing about...'

Teacher voice now, 'It says, and I quote, *"And any other duties as seen necessary for the needs of the service."* Emptying a paper bin is necessary. A full paper bin a fire risk. Close the door behind you please.'

And just fuck off you whiny little weasel.

***

By home-time, I was tired and incredibly snappy. I collected my youngest from the childminder and just longed for a bath. Instead, I had 3 rounds of homework to help with and 1 major cupboard search for last minute food tech ingredients.

I'd received several messages from Charlotte in-between her clients, Wilson was all things wonderful. Whilst I was genuinely happy that she had finally found a man worthy of her, it made me feel a bit shit. Andy hadn't bothered to message me, not even once.

The tournaments were due to start the following day and I'd be standing on the sidelines feeling invisible at this rate.

I told her, *"I thought he might have rung or even messaged by now,"* sad face emoji.

"I'll ask Wilson, make sure everything is ok, see if he knows anything!"

"Thanks. BUT don't tell Wilson that I know you're asking – don't want to look like a sad old cow, do I, lol."

Why I added a 'lol' I didn't know, the last thing I felt like was laughing out loud.

I had an early night. Self-pity had worn me out.

The next morning, I felt much the same. I'd dreamt of Clare and her high hair laughing at me as I walked in a short nightshirt and no knickers along the football field.

Christ, it was middle school all over again.

I used to dream that it was swimming day and I'd forgotten my costume so had to go all Emperor's New Clothes.

Work dragged. Jordan kept giving me bombastic side eye which, in the spirit of professionalism, I chose to ignore.

I had after all, survived my children's ninja death stares for years. Jordan's side eye was a gnat's knacker of concern by comparison.

I got back to my office and checked my phone, there was a message from school. *"Reminder to Parents: Tournament starts at 5pm. See you all there. Andy Gilmore."*

Oh. Ok. Not what I was hoping for.

I forwarded it to the coven chat, *"Just got this from Andy….. bit generic and from the schools' number, not his. Bad sign?"*

They agreed, generic and odd it was from the school and not him, but he was probably busy getting organised. It was a massive event in the school calendar.

That was true. It was a massive event for all the schools concerned. I convinced myself [briefly] that was why, he was just busy organising it.

I was owed some hours back at work, so I'd arranged to finish at lunchtime. There was no way that I was going to turn up to tournament looking like I'd spent the day in a skip.

An effort must be made. If I'd been cold shouldered, it would at least show Andy what he was missing. Of course, if I hadn't been cold shouldered, it would show Clare with the hair, that I could mean business too.

My eldest two children were staying at school until kick off, all I had to do was collect Finn from the childminder and get a parking space. The parking space was the difficult bit. I'd seen parents arrive at school an hour before they needed to be there, just to nick a parking spot. The concept of walking more than 50 feet was obviously alien to them.

I left the car parked at the vets' surgery, I'd spent enough money there in the past year and figured they owed me something back. Besides the vet recognised my car from the number of times she'd had to treat knob-dog in it. He demolished the surgery once in his eagerness to get out, so we'd agreed that unless it was life threatening, he'd be treated in the car.

Finn and I filed in through the gates like sheep and found a spot halfway along the pitch to wait. I'd spotted Wilson setting out bottles of water but couldn't see Andy anywhere.

'There he is!!' Finn suddenly yelled.

Looking up, I saw my eldest son lead his team out for the warm-up. Lexi was sat in the stands with her mates, I waved at them both.

Cal returned a half wave, and Lexi merely nodded like a gangster giving the signal for something murderous, and then turned her back on me.

Astounded by their overwhelming love, I consoled myself with the fact that at least the little one was still happy to be seen with me, for now.

The other team came out to warm up, led by a boy that couldn't possibly have been a Year 10. He was built like a brick shit house. Christ, I just hoped that he didn't run into my son, his collar bone would snap like a twig again.

I saw Andy as he made his way along the growing line of parents on our side of the pitch. My heart leapt. It felt like ages since I'd seen him. He happily greeted parents along the line,

'Hi, good to see you.'

'Thank you for coming.'

'Great to see you too,'

He finally got to me, 'Nice to see you.' and he moved on.

He just fucking moved along. No special greeting for me. Nothing. I got the same as Dennis the Menace stood next to me.

I saw Clare and her hair sneer at me as Andy continued his parental meet and greet.

Go suck a turd, you minging mare.

I sent a text to my non-related sister and told her what had just happened.

"Oh, that's fuckin harsh. Wilson didn't say anything either way. Hang in there. Focus on Cal."

That made me feel guilty. She was right, my son should be my focus, not the cold rejection that Andy had just delivered.

The whistle blew and the game kicked off.

I had to admit, despite Cal's best efforts, I didn't fully understand the rules of football, but it seemed that the sideline experts either side of me did.

They bawled at the ref, who was apparently illegitimate. They yelled at the touchline assistants, who were also of questionable parentage, and they yelled at Andy, who was allegedly a prick.

I couldn't argue with that particular sentiment.

Even Finn got involved with the shouting, although he questioned the ref's eyesight, rather than his parentage. Thank god.

At half time it was a frustrating 0-0.

Clare had moved her skinny self to stand next to me, 'Still seeing Andy? Jim, Mr Morgan to you, wasn't impressed when I spoke to him.'

My heart hammered, 'Have you really got such a shallow, sad fucking life that you need to try and fill it by shit stirring and gossiping about other people, Clare?' I spoke without bothering to look at her.

She snorted, 'I'm not the one with a sad life, mooning after a teacher.'

I leaned in as close as the thick thatch would allow and

whispered slowly, 'Fuck off Clare, before I put you on your bony arse.'

'You wouldn't dare!' she hissed.

I moved my youngest out of the way and turned to face her, I was taller than her and quite a few pounds heavier and I'd stopped whispering. 'You'd be wise not to test that theory. Now. Fuck. Off.'

She walked away.

My hands shook with adrenalin. I'd never wanted to deck someone as much as I had her in that moment. Not even my ex-husbands, and they'd deserved it a million times over.

'Mum! You said a swearing word!' Finn looked at me with wide eyes.

There was no denying it, 'I did. I'm sorry. As you grow up, you'll learn that some people need a swearing word to make them realise just how horrible they are.'

'Too right!' Dennis the Menace clapped me on the back, 'I hate that snotty cow.'

Well, at least I had one fan.

Andy stood on the pitch ten feet away. The look he gave me told me he'd witnessed all of that. Awesome.

The teams came back on, and the second half kicked off. The brick shit house kept gunning for my son, but his teammates were having none of it, and kept him out of Cal's way.

I'd bent down to tie my shoelace when a deafening roar went up. The boys had scored. Shit. I'd missed it.

The moment I stood up I knew who'd scored that goal. My son's team were all over him, clapping him on the back. Finn was cheering like a feral child.

I joined in on the woo-hoo's just as they were ending. I hoped my boy hadn't noticed that I'd missed his goal.

As it turned out, that was the only goal in the whole match. Brick shit house refused to shake hands with the opposing team and stomped off in a large tantrum.

Cal was a hero to his team. They were now through to the next game in 2 days' time.

Great. I had to do this all over again. I wondered what sly tricks Clare would have pulled by then. I wouldn't put it past her to have charmed Mr Morgan and got me banned.

Andy was lost in a sea of congratulations. I couldn't get near him.

My older two came running over, 'Can we go to Pizza Palace with the rest of the guys? Zane's mum said she'll drop us back home.'

'We can come with you, it'll be nice.' I offered.

'No, it's ok mum, it's just mates, not parents.'

That told me.

'Ah. Ok, see you later then.' I gave them both £20 and knew I'd never see the change.

***

At home, once Finn was tucked into bed, I rang the coven hotline and reported the events of the evening.

First and foremost, I told them that my eldest son was the school hero. Many congratulations went out to him and quite rightly, although they found it 'typical' that I'd missed the goal tying my laces.

I then told them about Andy's cold shoulder and Clare's nastiness.

'What a total bitch!' Sarah exclaimed. 'Sounds like she's gone running to the head and threatened Andy's job, doesn't it. She's jealous!'

We all agreed she was a bitch. It didn't help the overall situation at all though. Andy was still staying away from me, and I'd threatened Clare. Which, now that the heat of the moment had gone, I was shitting myself about.

If I got banned from the next game, I'd never be forgiven.

Date 27

As I waited for the older two kids to come home, I'd made my decision. I text Charlotte and asked her if she would please forward Wilson's number, I had to speak to him about Andy urgently.

As I have no patience whatsoever [another of my stunning qualities] waiting for her to respond felt like an eternity.

I logged back into the dating website. Was Wilson still on it now that he had my non-related sister? Crap. No. His profile no longer existed. I closed my account while I was in there. It just didn't seem right still having it sat there, with *or* without Andy. It had brought me nothing but misery, and I could watch a documentary on the cost-of-living crisis if I wanted to be miserable.

I rummaged through the drawer of discarded things in the kitchen. Every household had one. Filled with screwdrivers, pennies, broken pencils and, of course, letters and notes from school that parents thought they'd better keep, just in case.

It was the 'just in case', but never thrown away, pile of papers that I needed.

One very messy worktop later and I'd found what I was looking for. School had sent home an art exhibition flier, their very own Mr Wilson was displaying some of his work, they were very proud etc etc. The flier was almost a year out of date, but I hoped the mobile number on it was still in date and wasn't the organisers' number.

I didn't get the chance to try it, Charlotte had sent through his number, *"Hope he can help! Good luck, let me know!"* four leaf clover, heart emoji.

The number on the flier wasn't Wilson's, good job that in my desperation to get hold of him, I hadn't tried it.

Ignoring the heap of mess I'd made, I rang Wilson. He didn't pick up, so I left a rambling voicemail.

The kids arrived home full of laughter and joy. It was a refreshing change to see them so full of happiness, chatting away together. They headed for their respective rooms after each of them gave me a welcome and much needed hug.

My phone rang, Wilson.

'Hey, thanks for calling me back. I'm hoping you can help if you have 5 minutes to chat?'

Five minutes? Who was I kidding.

Fifteen minutes later, I'd finished my tale of War and Peace, took a deep breath and waited for Wilson's response.

'Okay. I haven't had the chance to speak to Andy properly, he's been organising the tournament, so I've hardly seen him. I'll ring him and see what he says,' he paused, 'and I'll give him your number if you don't mind, then you two can talk directly.'

I interrupted him, 'He's got my number, I gave him it at the Boathouse.'

Wilson laughed, 'Actually, you gave him the receipt for lunch.'

'No. I wrote my number on a piece of paper, I put it in my pocket...'

Shit. I knew what I'd done. I'd shoved the paper in my pocket along with the receipt and handed him the wrong one.

I told Wilson, 'I gave him the wrong bit of paper. Oh my god, I'm such a dickhead. It's no wonder he hasn't rung me.'

'Yeah, he kind of thought you were stringing him along.'

'No! No! I wouldn't do that, I genuinely thought I'd given him my number. I've been waiting to hear from him, and he never called and then, tonight, he blanked me. Oh, shit,' I couldn't believe what I'd done, 'Please, please tell him it was a genuine mistake!'

I realised I sounded like a child begging for an ice cream, so I shut up.

Wilson took a deep breath, 'Clare Thompson is a nasty piece of work,' he paused, 'and you should know that she's been trying to get Andy's attention for a long time. He can't stand her, but that hasn't stopped her throwing herself at him every opportunity.'

'What? She's married, isn't she?' I blurted.

'Separated I think, I've never paid much attention to her. She knows Jim Morgan pretty well though, so if she's stirring, she'll have an audience there.'

'Could Andy lose his job because we had lunch?' I had a feeling that Clare and her hair weren't finished with the nastiness.

'Nah, it's not a sackable offence to have lunch! Andy's not afraid to tackle Morgan either. Let me have a chat to him and I'll see if I can get him to ring you, ok?'

'Great, thanks!'

'I wish I'd have been there though when you threatened to deck her,' Wilson laughed, 'I bet her facelift slipped a bit.'

Ooooh, Wilson could be catty too!

I thanked him again and apologised for dragging him into my soap opera episode.

I updated the coven on my balls-up with the receipt and phone number, and that I was waiting to hear from Wilson, or better yet, Andy himself. I also told them that Clare had chased Andy and got nowhere.

"Told you! That's what this is all about, she's a fuckin jealous bag of bones!"

Yes. Yes, she is. Thank you, ladies.

By the time my eyes closed for the night, I hadn't heard from Andy or Wilson. Disappointed, I fell into a deep sleep undisturbed by dreams.

Work dragged the next day, mainly because I was on phone watch. Again. I poked the screen repeatedly to check for messages. There weren't any.

I felt miserable. Why didn't things ever work out the way they did in romantic comedies?

Because they're a pile of bullshit! Made to fool us into thinking that the world is a shiny, happy place where everything works out in the end.

Well fuck you rom-com genre. You're selling lies to lonely people who desperately want to believe in love. People who end up living their lives through the characters, who aren't real. People like….

Oh god. People like me.

***

I arrived home still feeling sorry for myself. My phone had stayed silent, even my mother hadn't bothered to call back.

I fed the kids, feigned interest in their social lives and headed out for an evening dog walk.

The dogs must have sensed my mood as they both behaved impeccably, even when a pair of over excited labradors bounded out of the woods ahead of us.

I sat on a tree stump, lost in a cloud of 'poor me' when my phone rang. Unknown number.

I answered it, 'Self-pity helpline, how may I help you?'

The lady trying to sell me the pet insurance renewal didn't try very hard. She sensed my lack of interest and said they would email.

Even she didn't want to talk to me.

The unknown number rang again, 'I thought you were emailing the quote over.'

'I can. What do you want a quote for? Personal liability insurance? Boxing glove replacement?'

Andy!

'Oh god, sorry, I thought you were the pet insurance! I'm so, so sorry I gave you the receipt, I thought it was my number and now I feel a total arse. I'm sorry.'

I think that covered it for the apologies.

'Can we have a chat, in person, if that's ok? You got a free half hour tonight?' He sounded distant.

I checked the time, 'Yeah. Of course. That would be nice.'

He didn't agree that it would be nice, instead he just said, 'Could you come to mine, I've got the kids tonight, their mum's not well, so they've come home early.'

He gave me his address. I had an hour to get changed and get there.

Under normal circumstances, I avoided all things running, but these weren't normal circumstances. I ran home with the dogs loving the fact that I'd gone exercise mad.

An hour later, I pulled up outside Andy's house. It was more of a smallholding than a house. I heard the yell of Bob the goat and the shouts of his feathered friends coming from the back. There was no sight or sound of the dogs.

One deep breath and a few 'you can do this' chants later, I'd knocked on the door and stood waiting.

Andy opened the door and gave me a half smile, 'Come in.'

I couldn't gauge his body language and was, quite frankly, shitting myself. If I was about to be unceremoniously dumped, that would have meant we'd been in some kind of relationship. If I was in for a bollocking for my near fight with Clare, then I'd lost a new friend.

He offered coffee, which I accepted. There was no sign of the kids. The kitchen was neat, tidy and HUGE. I felt like a pee on a drum as I perched on a bar stool next to the massive wooden table.

He plonked my coffee down and sat opposite me, which seemed a million miles away. 'I thought it would be better to talk face-to-face rather than over the phone.'

I nodded, 'Yeah, of course.'

Just get on with it man, if you're going to tell me to leave you alone and this was all a mistake, please just say it so I can grab my humiliation cloak, and leave.

He took a very deep breath, 'I thought we got on really well and I've enjoyed your company, even though you seemed disappointed that I wasn't your portion of vegetable rice.' He half smiled and looked so awkward.

I waited for the 'but'.

'Look, I'm just gonna say this, and it's not easy, so bear with me.'

Fucking hell, this was a serious talk, 'Okay.'

'I like you; I really like you and I thought maybe this could be something, *would* be something, but I've no idea how you feel. So, I'm asking, how do you feel?' He looked at me and waited.

For someone who's normally articulate, I just sat there. What was I supposed to say? Did I go for the truth and lay it all on the [huge] table, or did I try to keep some shred of dignity and skirt around the truth?

I played for thinking time while I took a sip of coffee. You're 53 woman, just tell him! At least that way, like the X-Files, the truth is out there.

Deep breath. 'Andy, I do like you. I mean, okay. You nearly deafened me, and you weren't vegetable rice, but I like you and I'm so sorry I fucked up the phone number thing. I can't imagine what you thought about that, well, I can, but it was a genuine mistake, and you know that and, well. Yeah, I really like you too.'

Super articulate.

I can't remember exactly what happened next. One minute I was sitting there like a bumbling buffoon and the next he was right there, kissing me. It was like I'd fainted for 20 seconds, and woken up, mid kiss.

He moved back, smiled and said, 'Glad that's sorted then.'

'Mmmmmm.' No words came out, just the sound you make when something is super tasty.

'You ok?' His hand still held mine as he moved his bar stool closer.

'Absolutely. Yep, all good. Great in fact.'

Get a fucking grip woman.

'There's something else I need to talk to you about,' the B&Q paint chart eyes lingered on my dirty pond algae-green ones.

Oh no.

'Clare Thompson.'

'Oh fuck. Yeah, erm, I sort of had a bit of a barny with her yesterday at the match.' I mumbled.

Andy laughed, a genuine, beautiful laugh that took me on a journey back to those missing 20 seconds…. Stop it!

'Yeah, I heard that. It was also the talk of the staff room, and the parent's piss-up.'

Crap. Had I turned into high school's Rocky Balboa or Ivan Drago? Was I the goody or the baddy?

I dealt with it as I did with many things, I lobbed some pathetic humour at it, 'Is she suing me? Do I need to leave the country under the cover of night and change my name to Doris Delooze? Tell me!'

'She couldn't sue you; you didn't actually do anything.' He paused, 'I think everyone was happy that someone dealt with her though. She's like mouldy marmite, not very popular. There's another thing, the dating a parent issue.'

Was he about to drop an atom bomb on our official 5-minute relationship?

I looked like a slack jawed llama, 'Okay.'

'Like I'd said, it's frowned upon, virtually banned and all that. Clare knew that and ran straight to Jim Morgan. Morgan and I have had a chat about it and it's fine, although the whole receipt thing nearly made me ask him to blacklist you from the PTA,' he smiled, 'I just didn't want you worrying about it. He'd appreciate us not flaunting anything in front of the school though. Bad image, conflict of interest and all that,' he lifted my chin up, 'Is that ok? Presuming of course that you want this, us, to be a thing.'

'Hell yeah! I think I can keep my clothes on when we're in public.'

Bloody hell, I said that out loud. Shit, shit, shit. 'I mean, absolutely. No snogging pitch-side.'

And that's how we had to leave it. A sleepy-eyed small person had wandered into the kitchen and held her arms out for a hug.

'I'd better go and leave you to it.' I whispered, 'See you tomorrow.'

I wasn't sure if I should have in front of the small person, but her eyes had closed again in her dad's arms. I reached up and kissed, well, I aimed for his cheek, but only managed to reach his chin. Fab.

Despite the chin kiss, I'd driven home in a cloud of 'Woo-Fuckin-Hoo's' and couldn't wait to tell the coven. I even had a glass of red wine to celebrate… on a school night too!

Cheers!

Date 28

If I'd have had a pervy person mirror on my bedroom ceiling, I'd have woken to see the massive grin on my face.

I'd dreamt of matching paint cards in B&Q to Andy's eyes. In my dream he'd happily stood there while I sang to him all of the colours I'd matched.

'You sad arse!' Charlotte cackled down the phone, 'You don't need a therapist to tell you what that means! You've been walloped by Cupid, right in the brain!'

'Well, maybe.' I attempted coy but managed smug instead.

'I'll see you tonight anyway, I want to see my nephew kick another goal and watch you batter Clare like a cod!'

She hung up.

As I was working from home, I didn't need to get dressed, not even for the school run. I just opened the car door and lobbed the kids out one by one, like an episode of The Fall Guy.

I'd got a couple of text pings on the way home, being a good law-abiding citizen, I didn't check my phone until I got back into the house.

Mother and Andy. Like the perfect daughter, I read Andy's first.

"See you at 5. Loved last night…. Especially the chin kiss. Awesome. Xx"

Pah! Pillock!

"Chin kiss intentional, I only save them for VERY special chins xx"

I read my mum's text, twice.

"Heard you've had an altercation with Clare Thompson….. We're in UK. Be with you about 2.30. Got my spare key. Mum."

Oh Fuck. How? How did she know I'd threatened Clare with the hair?

By 'we' I guessed Roger the dodger was in attendance. Bollocks. The house was a mess. Another benefit of working from home was that I could quickly hoover and tidy round in my 'coffee break'.

My lunch break was spent in the shower. I wasn't having another round of criticism about the state of my house *and* person, especially if I'd got a lecture on 'un-lady-like behaviour' coming too.

I'd messaged the coven and warned them that the mothership would be in residence, *"Avoid, avoid, avoid"*.

The childminder was taking the youngest to the match, her grandson was playing on the other team, so she was going there anyway. Great. That meant I had no excuse to cut my mother off.

They'd arrived in a Range Rover that was not my mum's. I waved in the general direction of the car and went to open the door after a battle to put knob-dog and his sidekick into the garden.

And there she was. A vision in lilac. Pristine as ever. Roger still looked the same dapper man we'd met in the spa, she hadn't drained the life out of him, yet.

Air kisses supplied, I got coffees and waited for the lecture to unfurl itself from her tongue.

'So, tell me what happened with Clare.' It wasn't a question.

I explained, in detail just what a vicious bitch she'd been and emphasised that it had all gone on whilst my beloved boy was playing a match that was *so* important to him. She took the hook.

'Well, well. We will have to see about her won't we.'

The way she said it unnerved me; she'd gone all Beth Dutton on me.

'Anyway, never mind her. Tell me about this Andy,' she leaned forward, ready to absorb it all.

I explained who he was and [very briefly] how we'd met initially and then how we'd properly met and waited for her scathing commentary.

'A dating site! Good God! That's tacky Freya, almost as tacky as speed dating. All the terrible things you hear about people on those things. I'm surprised you weren't mugged or swapped on the market for a few beans like Jack's cow!'

Roger patted her hand, 'There, there Eloise, all's well. She's found her beau now.'

I look at him and was grateful he was there to distract her.

'Of course, darling. You're right, as always.' They puckered up and exchanged lingering kisses.

Pass the puke bucket. Roger excused himself and headed for the bathroom, for a pee I hoped.

She turned to me, 'So, this Andy. He's Cal's teacher, yes?'

I nodded.

'And how does Cal feel about you sleeping with his teacher?' She raised a perfectly coloured eyebrow.

Shit. I'd been so wrapped up in Andy that I hadn't thought about how it might affect Cal.

'Well, I'm not, I haven't actually slept with Andy…and Cal doesn't know, yet,' was my pathetic self-absorbed defence.

'It might be an idea to tell Cal, don't you think? Before someone else does. If I know one thing about Clare fucking Thompson, she's too much like her mother. Vicious little bitch, she won't care who she hurts, and she'll take great delight in pissing on your parade. Darling.'

My mother's normal persona had returned in Roger's absence.

It dawned on me then, 'Is Margaret 'fucking' Thompson, Clare's mum?'

Roger appeared as I asked her.

'Don't swear darling, it's common. Yes. Yes, she is. So, you just watch that one.' She gave Roger her best smile, 'Well, we'd better get off, we need to book into the hotel. The game's at 5, yes? I'll see you there.'

And with that, they left.

I sat and stared at the empty sofa. What would Cal think? What if he got upset? He'd already voiced his dislike of my 'old people' dating efforts, how was he going to feel when he found out I was dating his sporting mentor?

I rang Sarah, 'Just be honest with him. Tell him how you feel about Andy and hopefully he'll be fine with it. You're entitled to have a life!'

Sarah was the oracle of all things parenting but she'd never had to tell her son that she was planning on banging his sports teacher.

'What if he goes mad? I can't tell him before the game, and if they win tonight, it's the final on Saturday. I can't tell him before that!' A mild panic had fallen over me.

She adopted her calm tone, 'Then don't. At the moment, there's nothing much to tell is there? You've shared a few drinks, lunch and a couple of kisses. He doesn't need to know about everyone you've locked lips with, does he!'

Reasonable. The list of frogs I'd kissed was very long indeed. He certainly didn't need to know about *that* list.

I looked at the clock, I needed to get ready and leave.

My phone pinged, Andy had sent a little red heart text, which I quickly returned with a kiss face.

***

I waved to the childminder. Finn had decided to stay with her to watch the match. I hadn't spotted my daughter but there were a gaggle of girls near the stands. She was probably with them.

Wilson and my non-related came and stood next to me.

'All sorted I hear,' Wilson winked at me.

Smug grin back, 'Seems so.'

I elbowed Charlotte, 'If looks could kill, you'd be 6 feet under, my lovely.'

I discreetly side-eyed in the direction of a gang of mums who had gone for the group death glare.

'Who are they?' she looked puzzled.

'Wilson's fan club.'

'Ignore them.' He told her and kissed her hand which was firmly held in his.

Andy appeared, 'I see you've upset your groupies.' His hand briefly brushed mine, 'See you all soon.' He winked at me and walked away.

'And Wilson's fans aren't the only ones upset.' Charlotte indicated to her right.

Clare and her hair stood with her arms folded, looking like she'd taken my advice, and sucked a turd.

My mother's perfume arrived before she did, 'Hello darling.' She air kissed Charlotte and introduced her to Roger.

As is polite, Charlotte introduced Wilson to my mother, 'Eloise, this is Zak. Zak, this is Eloise.'

'Pleasure.' My mum drawled as Wilson shook her hand.

A roar of cheers told me that the teams were making their way out. I saw my boy proudly leading his team out.

Mum dabbed her eyes in a rare emotional moment. She gripped Rogers' arm. Maybe she'd changed after all.

Almost immediately there was a goal. I proudly watched my boy congratulate his teammate. The roar was deafening. Andy nodded to the boys. Job well done.

At half time Roger went off with Wilson to get drinks.

Mum leaned over to us, 'He's bloody gorgeous.'

'Mine or hers?' Charlotte cackled.

'Both! Well done girls!'

I watched Andy wander away towards the changing rooms and felt lucky that he'd chosen me too.

'I wonder how long it'll be before he's in the arms of another woman. Bit of a track record of that happening to you, eh?' A nasal voice hissed beside me.

I recognised the poisonous tone before I'd even turned around.

'Did you not get the message the other night?' I couldn't be bothered to look at Clare.

'A little young for you, don't you think? He isn't going to stay...'

She didn't finish her sentence. My mum moved in between us, 'Clare dear. If you don't leave my daughter and *her* Andy alone, I'll happily announce in Sunday's paper just what it is your father really does for a living.' She leaned in closer to Clare, 'and we wouldn't want that getting out now, would we?'

Clare opened and closed her mouth like a goldfish.

In a louder voice my mum said, 'Goodbye Clare, it's been lovely to see you.'

Charlotte and I stared after Clare and looked back at mum. My mother had ripped the bullying bitch apart without so much as lifting a finger. Amazing move.

Roger and Wilson returned with drinks, completely unaware that my mum was an assassin.

As much as I tried to forget them, Clare's words stayed in my head. I leaned over to Wilson and tried to sound as light-hearted as possible, 'Can I ask you an odd question?'

'I don't like bananas and yes, I'm afraid of geckos.'

'Ha ha!.Nope, not that.' I paused, 'How old is Andy? Daft question I know, but it's never come up.' I tried to act like I hadn't a care in the world. I tried *really* hard.

He frowned, 'Erm, it was his 40th a couple of years ago, so 42- 43.' He winked, 'Remember, age doesn't count for diddly-shit.'

My mum interrupted, apparently, she was now an art enthusiast and needed Wilson's advice.

I suddenly remembered that Wilson had told me at the speed dating event, that age didn't count for diddly-shit. He was preparing the ground, the sneaky little sod!

Saying age didn't matter and believing it, were two

different things though. Andy was not only my football mad sons' sports teacher, but he was also about 10 years younger than me. What the hell was I going to do?

The teams came out for the second half, 'Here we go!' I said to no one in particular, and roughly shoved all the concerns to the back of my mind, determined not to miss any goals.

I couldn't miss them. There weren't any more.

Victorious, our boys won 1-0 which meant Saturday's final was on.

My kids came over to hug my mum, 'Are you going to be here for the final, momma?'

They called her momma because she refused to be called Grandma, Granny or Nanna, those particular titles all made her feel old apparently, and she *wasn't* old.

'Of course I will be my little ducklings. Roger and I have booked in at the hotel all weekend, I knew you'd get through!'

Introductions to Roger were easy, the kids seemed to like him.

'Now, let me take you all for food, how about Mexican or Chinese? There's a gorgeous looking Chinese restaurant next to our hotel.'

With a resounding yes, the kids wandered off with my mother to get ready for their meal.

Yeah. I bet there were more than 2 cubes of food for them. She'd offered to take me as well, but I declined and used the excuse that I still had work to do, I didn't. I needed to speak to Andy.

I could see him surrounded by the parent squad, all praising him. It always made me laugh how fickle fans of any sport, were. They were all over a team and their coach when they were on the up, but if they lost, the players and the coach were suddenly every tit wanking dickhead under the sun.

I waited until the seething mass of handshakes had moved off and I moved in. 'Hey, I know you're super busy, but I wondered if I could pinch you for a bit?'

Even sweaty, Andy looked amazing. I was suddenly very aware of his youthful looks.

'I need to go and confirm Saturday's arrangements. I've got to let the entertainment and caterers know final numbers. Can we catch-up later?' His phone rang, 'Ah, speak of the devil, I'll ring you later, ok?' He winked at me and wandered off chatting on the phone.

I stood there as he walked away. I'd forgotten about Saturday. My son had shoved the invitation in my hand some weeks before and although I registered it at the time, so much had happened since, that I'd forgotten.

There was a big 'End of the Season' event planned. Suddenly, it felt more than just the 'End of the Season'.

Date (ish) 29

I'd no idea how the hell I was going to get past my stress head, or even if I could. I drove back home a lonesome Joe and just felt shitty.

No matter how hard I tried to ignore it, Clare had a point. My 3 husbands had all cheated on me. Maybe there was something about me that sent them into the arms, or knickers, of other women. Would it be the same with Andy?

With no kids needing me, I hooked the dogs onto their leads and set off for a walk. As I wandered along, I played things over in my mind.

My decision to start dating again had been made on the back of a long road of self-understanding. Deep down, I knew I wasn't responsible for the actions of my husbands. It had taken time to accept that.

I was, however, responsible for my choice to be with them, and for my reactions to their actions.

I'd chosen to be with them, I'd chosen to get married at 20 despite warnings from my parents, but of course, I'd known better. I hadn't. He'd buggered off after 2 months of marriage with a Barbie look-a-like at Monsters of Rock, while I was watching AC/DC.

4 years later I got married for the second time. A week after our first anniversary, I'd come home from work early after breaking a finger under a 5-kilo Costco tub of margarine, only to find him happily screwing the neighbour. I never touched margarine or my husband again.

Finally, I'd married number 3 after I'd found out that I was having the twins. I thought it was the right thing to do. The possibility of bringing up twins on my own had frightened the fuck out of me, so I'd pushed the alarm bells away. Seven years later, thinking I'd got food poisoning, I'd discovered I was having another small human. Five years after bonus baby, my husband and his Pound Shop Kardashian got caught in the back of my Land Rover….in McDonald's car park, by Rachel's husband, Ben.

I got rid of the husband, but kept the Land Rover …. after a thorough and *very* deep clean.

That was my life. Filled with terrible choices and a small number of divorces.

Whilst I had no intention of ever getting married again, I didn't want to make another terrible choice. My heart just couldn't take it.

I'd wandered down to the woods and sat on the grass against the tall fence. Both dogs settled at my side. I was lost in a world of my own when knob-dog suddenly got excited.

'Been face-planting again?' Wilson said. With the rat on the lead, he stood on the other side of the fence.

He clicked his fingers and knob-dog sat.

'How do you do that? I can't get him to sit for a bloody steak, never mind a click of the fingers!'

'I worked in a rescue centre while I was at Uni, picked up all sorts of tricks. I can even pee standing on one leg.' He laughed, 'What are you doing here?'

I sighed, 'Contemplating my naval, lamenting life and pondering possibilities.'

'Blimey, bit deep for a Thursday evening. Sundays are usually reserved for that kind of reflection. What's up?'

The dogs hadn't moved, knob-dog sat looking at Wilson like he was a rock star.

'Just something Clare with the hair said, it's just made me think about things.'

'Clare with the hair?!' Wilson found that amusing, 'What venom did she spew this time?'

I told him her summary of my future.

Wilson sat at the other side of the fence. 'Look, the past shapes us but you can't let it define you. You learn from it and move on. You can't let it taint your future and you *can't* judge Andy on the actions of those worthless pricks.'

I smiled, 'Yeah. You're right. Thanks.'

He stood up, 'Is that all for this week's episode of 'Broken Hearts' or is there more?'

'Nah. No more, the audience is bored of my whining.' I nodded to the dogs who'd laid down.

Wilson nodded, 'Right, I've got a date with a beautiful lady and a bottle of red. See you Saturday!'

I waved him away, 'Go! Get out of here Romeo. Enjoy the wine!'

The kids arrived home after stuffing their faces.

'Don't you feed the poor things? They were positively starving!' My mother declared as she did the doorstep drop.

I kept my face straight and replied, 'I try not to; it just makes them crap more and I can't afford the toilet roll.'

My mum ignored that, 'I'll see you all Saturday. I take it I have an invitation to the End of Season Ball'.

'Erm, it's more of a disco and DJ job mum. I didn't know you were going to be here, so I haven't got you one.'

'I don't need one, I need two. Roger wants to see his grandchildren celebrating too. Sort tickets out for me please.'

Right. Roger had assumed grandfather status, had he.

My phone rang, Andy.

'I've got to take this mum. I'll see you Saturday.'

I closed the door and went into the kitchen. 'Hey, how's it all going?

'Yeah good. Be better if I could see you though. Fancy a kitchen coffee? Maybe this time you could aim a little higher than my chin.'

Hmmm, or a LOT lower. Gah, stop it you filthy mare.

'I'll be there at 8.'

I bribed the older 2 with a fiver each to babysit their brother for an hour or so while he slept and told them their aunty needed my sage advice on something.

***

One quick freshen up later and I headed to Andy's. I'd decided not to tell him about Clare's spew of bile, he didn't need the hassle, and I didn't really want to remind him of my many failed marriages.

He was at the door waiting and greeted me very differently this time, which suited me perfectly. Our romantic moment was interrupted by one of his dogs greeting me, right in the crotch.

The other dog, an old soldier, ambled in slowly. At least I could greet him before he reached my nethers. The first dog rounded and sniffed again, then sneezed loudly.

Before I engaged my brain, my gob spoke, 'I like to pepper the steak before a good sniffing.'

Mortified wasn't the word.

Andy didn't miss a beat, 'Good job I'm not vegetarian then.'

Good god! I quickly changed the subject, 'My mum needs two tickets for the End of Season supremo, is that possible?'

'Yeah, I've got a few spares. Coffee?'

'Thanks.'

I sat with my coffee and watched him while he talked about arrangements for Saturday. The game was set for 12pm and no matter the outcome, win or lose, the evenings celebrations would start at 6pm.

He handed me the tickets, 'It'll just give everyone a chance to wind down a bit before the evening kicks off. God, I hope they win, they've worked so hard. Especially Cal after his accident.'

Right, it was now or never, 'About Cal. My mum asked me how he felt about us, and obviously, I haven't said anything to him yet. I'm not going to until after Saturday because...'

'You don't know how he's going to take it?' he finished my sentence.

I nodded, 'Exactly. I hadn't even thought about saying anything at all for a while, until we were sure this was going to work,' I paused, 'But, as mum quite rightly pointed out, somebody else might.'

'By somebody else, you mean Clare?' He frowned, 'That's a fair point. How are you gonna feel if Cal gets upset? I don't know why he would though, but if he did…'

God, all the second guessing was stressful. 'In all honesty, I don't know how any of them will react, but it affects Cal more directly, obviously.'

He came over and hugged me, 'Let's cross that bridge when we get to it, eh?'

I agreed, lobbed it in the vault of my mind and then spent a very pleasant hour in his company.

***

At home, I got a text from Charlotte, *"You ok? Zak said you'd been upset by trout face's comments. Hugs and loves."*

"I'm fine thanks. Now piss off back to your perfect man and your perfect wine, you perfect bitch!"

She replied with two hearts and a turd. I replied with a middle finger emoji.

I spent the remainder of the evening chatting to the twins. Lexi had decided that a new dress was needed for Saturday, because *everyone* was wearing a new dress. She'd already arranged with my mum to go shopping straight from school the following day.

'Momma said she was gonna buy it for me, as a treat.'

Good, she could spend my mother's money instead of mine. 'Don't forget you'll need new shoes to go with it, and maybe new earrings.' I told her.

'Ooooh, yeah. I forgot about shoes and stuff. Thanks!' She rushed off to text my mum.

'Aren't you getting anything new?'

Cal was absorbed in his phone, he looked up frowning, 'Nah, I've got stuff in my wardrobe from prom, that'll do.'

And with that he said goodnight and disappeared.

I wondered what the hell I was going to wear. Had I got anything that I hadn't already worn? One rummage in my wardrobe later and I had to admit defeat. My wardrobe used to be crammed with clothes in a clear chain of command. Going out/smart but cool/smart work/garden and dog walking clothes.

For the past 3 years, I'd hardly gone anywhere, so most of the going out clothes had become smart work ones, which had now faded and never been replaced. Almost everything in my wardrobe was now either work, or dog walking stuff.

I'd exhausted the remaining going out clothes on the recent dates.

I had to face it. I needed to go shopping.

I bloody hated shopping, for anything, but especially clothes shopping. The whole experience was stressful. Clothes just weren't made for real bodies, especially ones like mine that were quite top heavy.

Women paid thousands for big boobs but if you had the big boobs/smaller bottom half combo, you were screwed. Nothing ever fitted properly. You were either squashed in and feared a hulk style top ripping, or clothes just hung around, like a maternity smock. Not flattering.

The thought of shopping was not a happy one. I messaged Sarah, *"I need to go clothes shopping. Nothing to wear that hasn't already been worn. Sorry."*

I knew what her response would be, and I was right.

"Oh shit. No tantrums this time. We'll find something. Ok??"

I couldn't promise, but I'd try.

***

After work, we met in shopping centre hell. I was one of those shoppers who knew what they liked and what they didn't, so I walked in and out of a shop in about 30 seconds flat.

'Nope. Nothing I like, it's all ugly or made for teens.'

After the third shop, she'd got pissed off.

'Right, we're going in here and you WILL find something or we're going home!' After years of experience, Sarah knew exactly how to handle my tantrums.

She'd collected an armful of brightly coloured things and bundled me into a changing room. I usually stuck to black and nothing else. Brightly coloured was going to be… interesting.

'Here, try this one first and then this.'

There was no arguing with her, she ignored my feeble protests that yellow was a hideous colour and matched my teeth, 'Just try it on!'

I looked like a daffodil. She agreed. 'It's bloody awful. Right, next!'

The blue dress was nice, but I couldn't get the zip done up past my bra strap.

'Let me try.' She yanked it around, 'Shit. Take it off. Quick'

I knew what had just happened.

'Right, these next. Go!'

The black lace top hugged me so tightly that the fabric became see-through.

'Not suitable for a school event, you look like Madonna in her Vogue video. Take it off.'

I held up the dark red dress she'd given me. Nice but it wouldn't fit. I tried it on and threw back the curtain.

Sarah clapped her hands in triumph, 'Yes! That's perfect! Look, go, there's a long mirror there.' She pointed to the end of the changing rooms.

It was really nice BUT it was, as my mum would have said, very booby. It clung to them, around them and on them like a vacuum-packed pair of melons. Elsewhere, the dress flowed elegantly like a gentle waterfall to my knees.

'That's the one! Take it off.'

Yes Ma'am.

'You've got those nice black heels, they'll go perfectly.'

This was exactly why I'd needed Sarah; she knew all things about shopping and clothes. I was hopeless.

We made our way to the till; I spotted Clare walking towards us. There was nowhere to hide.

She came up wearing her false smile and sneered, 'Oh, hello. I'm shopping for something fab to wear tomorrow night. I'll be bringing *my* date.' She sailed past us in a cloud of expensive perfume.

'Jesus. That smells like cat piss. I take it that's Clare and she thinks she's managed to split you and Andy up?' Sarah was very perceptive indeed.

I nodded.

'Well, she's going to be disappointed, isn't she!'

As we approached the till, Sarah found an assistant and handed over the blue dress and innocently told her, 'The zip on this is broken I'm afraid, I know you can't sell damaged goods, so I thought I'd better let you know.'

Wow! Just wow.

Date 30 (and big game)

I'd been thinking…. Clare was bringing a date to the end of season shindig. Hopefully that meant she'd leave me and Andy alone and wouldn't ruin the evening. One thing less to stress about.

Cal was up early and wanted to join me on the dog walk, which was lovely, but it meant he was nervous. Understandable.

I yabbered away to him, told him about his aunt's destruction of the zip and subsequent pretence that she'd found it that way. I then told him about Jordan and the paper basket rebellion, before I mentioned the coming match.

'Whatever happens, you've bounced back from injury and scored the goal that got us through in the first place. You're incredible! All of you are. You'll play your hearts out and make us proud, either way. We're already so proud.' I felt like Gareth Southgate preparing the team for their swift exit from the Euro's.

'Thanks mum. I know all that,' he chewed his lip, 'Backhouse are a tough team though, they slaughtered Longley on Thursday, absolutely crushed 'em. Elliot's letting things get to him, Mo and Hinkler are feeling the pressure too.' He sighed.

Mo and Hinkler? Sounded like a firm of solicitors.

'You're all feeling it, that's perfectly natural, it means you care and that's the important bit. You want me to give the pre-match pep talk? I'm good!'

'Bloody hell mum, no way!' he laughed and imitated me, 'Boys, listen up, you're amazing, I'm so proud of every one of you. Now, go out there and kick the fecking shit out of them.'

'Hey! I don't sound like that!'

'Yeah, you do.'

At least he was laughing now and for the sake of the match, I ignored his swearing.

We got home, he stopped before going to get a shower, 'Thanks mum. I needed that.'

Yes! One Mum of the Year award in the bag for me.

Cal eventually came out of the shower honking of Lynx and dumped his bag in the hallway, 'Zamir's mum's here,' he gave me a lopsided grin, 'See you soon, love you.'

'Come here,' I pulled my boy in for a hug, he was way taller than me but was never going to be too big for a hug, 'I love you too. See you soon. Say hi to Saffi for me. And Cal…'

'Yeah?'

'Kick their feckin arses baby.'

'We will!' he shouted over his shoulder and made his way out.

Of his sister, Lexi, there was no sign. She'd bought a dress with my mum but refused to show me until she was 'all done up, that way you'll see the full effect'. Fair enough. That worked both ways, I wasn't showing her my dress either, not that she was bothered what her mother was wearing, of course.

My youngest darling had wrecked the kitchen. He'd inherited my lack of coordination and spilt Shreddies all over the worktop and floor. Knob-dog and his sidekick were on it like flies on shit.

'Sorry!' he called as he climbed up onto the breakfast bar stool and slopped milk all over the floor.

He had the same 'it's a café' attitude as his siblings.

***

Much to the annoyance of Lexi, I decided that we were going to walk to the game. I knew there'd be no chance of parking. My daughter had her nose stuck to her phone all the way there.

'Watch the lamp-post!' I yelled. She almost gave herself a couple of black eyes to compliment her mystery dress.

No reaction. She swerved and carried on, glued to the little screen that seemed to be the life-force of all things social.

People and cars were everywhere. Idiots had parked so far up the pavement that it was a single file job to get past. My bag grated against a posh yellow car. Shit. It had scratched the glossy paintwork.

'Mum!' Lexi had managed to drag herself away from her phone in time to witness the bag attack.

'Well, they shouldn't have parked there, should they? A wheelchair or a pushchair would never get past.' I tried to justify my car scarring and point the blame stick at the car owner.

Finn piped up, 'It's their own fault mum.'

'Yes, my child, it's their own fault.'

Pitch side was rammed with parents, teachers and people I didn't recognise, hyped up, waiting for the game to start. The guy stood at the back of the group rustled in a blue carrier bag, pulled out a can of Carling and popped the lid.

Really? It's a school football match for fuck's sake.

I spotted the coven stood with my mother on the other side, manoeuvred Finn around boozy Bill, and headed their way. Lexi went to hang out with the 'cool crowd' in the stands.

'I can't believe the guy over there is on the beer!' I told them when I reached the group.

'Bit out of order at a kid's match, I'll keep an eye on him.' Roger had obviously decided he was on security for the day.

My mum smiled at him proudly and then asked, 'How was Cal this morning?'

I told them about the dog walk, 'He seemed more relaxed when we got back though.'

'Oh, here we go!' Rachel's husband Ben was covered in kids, one on his back and one on each hip. They'd adopted a trio of siblings four years ago and it had changed their lives, for the better. I'd never seen them so happy... or so covered in glitter and poster paint.

The teams followed Andy and the other coaches onto the pitch to a huge swell of cheers. The kids screamed in excitement. Even my mother bellowed like a water buffalo.

Cal's team waved without looking into the crowd, their eyes firmly on Andy. My boy looked like he meant business, his face said they were taking no prisoners.

The ref got on with the coin toss, indicated the direction and blew her whistle. Wilson and Charlotte stood hand-in-hand. Wilson's children were tucked either side of them. They made a lovely little family.

I wondered if we'd look like that someday, Andy and me, one super-sized family. My daydreaming was interrupted by a roar from the other side of the pitch. The other team had scored. Shit.

'It's not over until the large lady warbles. C'mon lads!' Roger was certainly getting into this. His tanned neck strained against his dapper collar and tie.

Indeed Roger. Come on lads!

Half time and they were still 1-0 down. The boys wandered away to the changing rooms; I could see Cal trailing behind them.

I sent a silent prayer to the god of all things football.

Sarah elbowed me, 'Isn't that mop man?' she indicated to down the line of parents.

I'd forgotten all about mop-man, it seemed a million years ago that I'd suffered that particular scary episode, 'What? Where?' I couldn't see him.

'There! Standing next to Clare and the guy in the red baseball cap. There!' She'd started to look like a nodding dog.

I looked down the pitch, I could see red cap man and Clare but not…. Holy shit! Yep, that was mop man. I tried to shrink back behind Wilson and his beautiful family. Fuck, what was he doing here? I couldn't see his feet [thank god] but the image of those grubby Gruffalo talons were embedded in my memory forever.

'What's up?' Charlotte had leaned back.

I mouthed, 'Mop man?'

She repeated, 'Mop man? Where?'

I pointed over like I'd grown a chicken wing.

She turned back to me, mouthed 'Oh fuck' and vomit mimed, 'What's he doing here?'

I shrugged.

The second half started. Mop man moved away down the line towards the drinks stand and I relaxed a bit. What the hell was he doing here? I hoped I hadn't got a stalker.

One of the other team had brought Mo down heavily in front of their goal. The ref blew for a penalty.

The other team's supporter's booed and called the decision various bags of shite, but she was having none of it. The penalty stood.

Mo recovered from his winding. I watched as Cal went over and spoke to him, nodded and moved away. Mo was taking the penalty and set the ball up. The other-side supporters heckled the poor lad.

It takes a special kind of shithead to heckle a 15-year-old kid. Wankers.

Mo must have had nerves of steel because he took the shot and scored. Yes! Cal and his comrades flew round Mo. I swear the ground shook.

Now that they were equal, you could see that the fire in their eyes had return.

Mo had flown down the pitch again. Getting flattened by the dirty player had obviously pissed him right off, and the adrenalin had given him super speed. The kid was like a cross between The Flash and a greyhound. Cal charged down with him. Two players blocked Mo's sight of the goal, he passed back to Cal who took the shot and smashed it home.

All around me erupted. 'Top bins!' 'Good Lad!'

I had no idea what 'top bins' meant but presumed it was good.

The remaining ten minutes were tense, the threat of Backhouse School scoring an equaliser made me feel sick.

Time suspended itself like a sloth, going nowhere fast. Everyone around me repeatedly checked their watches.

Finally, the whistle blew, and they'd bloody done it. They'd won the tournament! My youngest shrieked like a thing possessed and ran onto the pitch before I could grab him. He charged into the throng to find his big brother. Fearing for his life under the bouncing boots of celebration, I started to run after him, but Andy got to him first and lifted him safely out of the way.

'This one of yours by any chance?' he laughed and delivered my hollering boy.

Ahhhhh, my hero!

Andy was then swept away by a sea of cheering parents.

We made our way to the benches where the boys were maturely shaking hands with their crestfallen oppo's. I'd waited until they were all done and then, not caring who saw, grabbed my boy and gave him a life-threatening squeeze. Swiftly followed by his siblings, Cal untangled himself from his family fan club.

'Awesome job. I knew you'd do it!' I told him, my face hurt from the grinning.

My mum and my friends muscled in next, 'Oh my darling boy, you'll be playing in the professional leagues next. What a super-star!' my mum gushed at him.

We saw Clare standing next to her son, Elliot.

'Well done, Elliot, incredible job!' I told him. Not even Clare and her hair were going to spoil this for the boys.

'Thanks!' Elliot grinned and jumped away in celebration with another player.

Clare gave a cold smile.

Mum had moved to stand next to me, 'You must be proud Clare dear. Don't forget our little talk, it would be a shame to have to rename the cup.'

The cup? Shit, I'd forgotten about that. The Thompson Cup, sponsored by none other than Clare's dodgy dealings dad.

My mum was deadly. I was suddenly very proud of her.

The cup was to be awarded in the evening's celebrations.

In the name of all things politically correct, the school had decided that it would be bad form to lift it and gloat directly over the losing team. Although, it never seemed to bother Brazil that much.

It took another hour to get the boys off the pitch and out of the changing rooms. We'd planned to meet at mum's hotel for drinks before going to the shindig. She'd arranged a minibus apparently. Fab, it meant I might even be able to sneak a drink in the grown-up's bar later.

We'd headed back home; my daughter was over the moon. Cal's celebrity status meant she was getting lots of attention too.

As we got to the pavement pinch point, I saw mop man, I suddenly lobbed myself backwards into the bushes.

'What the hell?' Lexi looked at me like I'd lost the plot.

'Shhhhh. Come here, all of you. Quick!' I gestured that my offspring should join me in the foliage. Not one of them moved.

Finn held his hand out, 'What are you doing mum?

Why are you in the bushes?'

Bless him, my youngest was adorable, but he had one volume, not quiet.

Mop man was now getting into the posh yellow car that I'd scratched. Shit. I didn't think he'd seen me though.

Moments later, he drove off and I untangled my hair from an enthusiastic bramble.

'Was all that 'cos you scratched that car?' my daughter helped to pick the leaves out of my nest head.

'Well. Yes and no.' In an edited version, I explained about mop man.

'OH MY GOD! Gross!' she shrieked.

'I know, I know but I blocked him. I don't know what he was doing at the match though. He said he didn't have kids.' I was talking as much to myself as I was to my kids.

'Not that! The fact you were dating….online dating! Gross!' She pulled a face like she'd stepped in dog shit.

'Didn't you know she was on a dating site?' My cup winning son shrugged and set off on the now clear pavement.

'What? No! How did YOU know? Why didn't you tell me?' Lexi ran after him.

Yeah, how did you know and why didn't you say anything?

Date 31 [Important one]

I was chuffed to bits for the team. The walk home was so nice, none of the usual arguments or stomping off in a huff. Everyone was on a cup winning high.

As we only had 1 bathroom and there were 4 of us, of course everyone else called dibs and left me waiting until last.

Andy messaged me, *"What a finish! On a total high, can't wait to see you later and…"*

I didn't get to read the rest, Cal came in, 'Mum, she needs you, something about a hair disaster.' He shrugged.

I went in like the coiffure cavalry and saved the day with a million hairgrips and a tonne of hairspray.

'Thanks mum, you've not done a bad job,' Lexi was taking selfies of the back of her head.

'No worries, just don't go near a naked flame.' I gestured an explosion, 'Pooft.'

She looked at me and pulled her teen face, 'Whatever mum.'

With my hairdressing services no longer needed, Lexi shoo'd me out of her bedroom and closed the door.

Finally, it was my turn for the pamper preparations.

I looked in the bathroom and sighed. There was a purple ring around the bath from madame's bath bomb, hairs that I didn't even want to think about and a pair of dirty boxers to deal with, before I could get in the shower.

Kindly, they'd left me with one dry towel…. a hand towel.

I made sure that I used the expensive products that I'd hidden from my daughter. Experience had taught me that she 'borrowed' everything and never returned it until it was empty. I covertly used the treasured 'good stuff' and emerged from the shower smelling delicious.

I could hear the older two chatting and laughing downstairs, they were currently besties, that would last until at least tomorrow.

My hair behaved and for once, I didn't poke myself in the eye with the mascara wand. This was going well so far.

I teamed the new dress with my favourite heels and looked in the mirror. Not bad, not bad at all!

I'd never felt like a million dollars, but I sure felt a million pennies right now and that was good enough for me.

My daughter looked stunning, she really had become a beautiful young woman, but god help whoever she ended up with, high maintenance was going to be her life-motto.

Finn had taken Roger's advice and gone for a shirt and tie. In his beautifully unique way, he'd paired it with his favourite orange shorts and SpongeBob Converse.

Never change kid.

My superstar eldest son had his prom suit on, minus the jacket, 'Looks cooler with just the waistcoat,' he told me. Fair point. He looked incredible.

For my efforts, I got a 'bro yeah' [daughter] 'gorj' [big son] and 'soooo beautiful' [small son, and the only one I immediately understood]

The dogs had been banned to the kitchen; dog slobber was not required on our gorgeousness.

Roger picked us all up for the short journey to the hotel. I read Andy's text in full and held back a dirty laugh, *"Ready, willing and very able to help you with that! Xx"*

'You look happy mum.' Cal smiled at me.

'I'm happy because of you, *all* of you.'

The heartwarming moment was completely spoilt by a foul waft of arse gas. Roger discreetly rolled the windows down.

My daughter retched, 'Urgh, god. You dirty minger, who did that?'

'Christ, someone needs to wipe and flush.' Even Cal struggled with this one.

'That was me!' Finn proudly announced.

Yorkshire's answer to the Royle Family had hit the road.

***

Mum met us in the lobby dressed like a golden age Hollywood starlet, 'Darlings! You all look magnificent.'

She turned to me, 'And Freya, you've made an effort, wonderful to see.'

I wasn't sure if that was an insult or a compliment, so I let it go.

We were ushered into a private room where a waitress gave the adults champagne and the kids alcohol-free cocktails.

'To my darling boy and his victory!' Mum raised her glass to Cal.

Indeed.

I'd never seen my mum in love. Growing up, it had largely been the two of us. My father seemed to come in and out of our lives as he pleased, blaming his work commitments for his absence. Even on family holidays, he would disappear quicker than a con man when the bill arrived.

The problems started when he *was* around. Mum had spent so long being on her own that she didn't know how to be part of a marriage. When he retired, he expected her to let go of everything she'd become and accommodate her husband. She tried…. For about 2 weeks. They were strangers with a piece of paper, so she'd divorced him.

Roger had allowed my mum to be herself. It probably helped that he had a small fortune behind him, but somehow, I honestly believed that even if he didn't have a yacht, she'd love him anyway.

I hoped that Michael could see that too.

***

When the mini-bus arrived, it wasn't *actually* a mini-bus, it was a stretch limo, complete with a chauffeur. Blimey, mum really had gone all out.

'Roger's treat,' she told us proudly.

We all thanked Roger. He'd just scored another set of gold stars from the kids.

Drinks were available in the limo too. I could get used to this. I discretely leaned into my youngest boy and whispered, 'Please don't trump in here.'

He gave me a thumbs up and happily chugged his fruity mocktail. Two swift drinks in and we arrived at the End of Season extravaganza.

Andy was greeting everyone as they arrived, alongside Jim Morgan, the headteacher. Andy looked like he could out-Bond 007, my heart leapt.

Phwoar and fucking phwoar indeed!

Mr Morgan was not, and never would be phwoar. He just looked greasy and slicked back.

Morgan greeted Cal like his very best buddy, he was proud, so proud of all 'his boys', etc, etc.

Greasy Morgan then greeted my chest first, and me second, 'Very pleased to see you. I've heard a lot about you.' He briefly looked at Andy who was also staring, but at all of me, not just the boobs.

I replied insincerely to Mr Morgan, 'Hi. Nice to see you.'

And held back the… not really. You pervy old prick.

Andy however, I greeted with a far more sincere and lingering hello.

It took a few moments to get through the elderly security chap, he squinted at each invitation like it was a passport checkpoint. Eventually, we made it through the FBI reject's control station and wandered in.

***

Instructions for the evening were clear. No alcohol was allowed in the main auditorium where the young people would be, and the young people were not allowed in the adult-only bar.

We found our table; the team had their own table front and centre. The kids all wandered off to be with their friends and show off their outfits. The huge dance floor was empty apart from the odd floating evil balloon. We still had 25 minutes before the official start of the celebrations,

Mum and Roger were deep in conversation, I had time. I excused myself to the back of their heads and wandered off towards the adult bar.

The coven had arrived, along with Wilson, I waved and indicated where I was headed. They didn't need telling twice. Wilson had teacher duties, so kissed his belle and disappeared.

Sadly, it wasn't a free bar, it was a bloody expensive bar. One small wine later and I was down almost a tenner. Feckin hell, I hoped there was more than moths in the bank, or I'd be on toilet water.

We'd all congratulated each other on how awesome we looked, when Charlotte mumbled, 'Incoming. Two o'clock.'

Clare came into view in the daffodil dress I'd rejected. Her hair was piled so high on top of her head, it reminded me of a huge blonde horse turd.

'Evening,' Clare then eyed my group and looked my dress up and down. An arm moved at the side of her and handed her his drink, he glanced our way briefly and disappeared towards the toilets clutching his phone and unzipping his fly.

Clare sneered in our direction and turned away, trying to balance her drinks whilst trotting after her date. Sarah almost choked on her expensive wine.

Clare's date was none other than mop man.

'Holy crap, that's why he was at the match!' she started laughing.

I couldn't believe it, 'Wow! At least he didn't recognise me, and look…..she's finally found someone deserving and worthy of her. Awwww.'

We were still laughing as the ceremony began. The main lights dimmed, and the stage lit up like Blackpool illuminations. In a monotone voice, Mr Morgan took centre stage, the lights glaring off of his greasy head. He wittered on about how team spirit was so important and how proud *he* was to be behind such a successful team.

'And, without further ado, I'll let our sports leader and highly regarded coach, Andy Gilmore, take it from here.'

Oh yes. Please do, he's far more interesting.

Andy approached the podium looking completely and utterly phwoar, 'Good evening.' He had to wait a good 5 minutes for the applause to die down.

'Thank you. When I first came to the school, there was very little in the way of equipment, facilities or even footballs!' he gave a clear side glance at Morgan, 'Thanks to the national initiatives and local community leaders, we managed to get everything we needed, but,' he paused to look at the team, 'We are only here tonight, celebrating, because of the teams, because of the young people. Their enthusiasm, tenacity and heart are what have made it a success. You can throw all the money in the world at a problem but without these young people, it's just worthless paper. I'm so proud of each, and every one of them.'

God, he was good.

'Ladies and gentlemen, please welcome to the stage, your team.' Andy called them to stand alongside him.

The room broke into rapturous applause, my mum and Roger whistled and whooped-whooped like they were at a rave. Oh, what the hell, I joined in.

Cal and his team nudged each other in happiness. Mr Morgan slimed his way back across the stage like a giant slug, carrying the cup.

'Ladies and gentlemen.'

Noone listened; the cheers continued.

Louder then, 'Ladies and gentlemen,' he waited as the room eventually silenced, 'It gives me great pleasure to award the Thompson Cup to our very own Edenthorpe boys under 16's.'

The room roared again. I watched my son lift the cup and clapped until my hands went numb. Cal passed the cup along; each player lifted it to renewed applause.

I felt a hand on my back and turned to see Andy standing there.

I got my aim right this time and gave him a quick kiss on the cheek. He whispered in my ear, 'You look fucking stunning.'

There were shouts of 'Mr Gilmore,' 'Andy.' It was photo time, he moved off to get the official team photos taken. I saw the coven gesturing to the bar. I didn't need asking twice.

'That was awesome! Did you see Cal's face? He was so proud! And....I think he's got a girlfriend...' Rachel nodded like a know-it-all.

'What? Which one?' he'd kept that quiet.

'Pretty little thing in the pink dress. I'll show you when we go back in. Now, cheers!'

We raised our glasses together as Clare came into to the bar like an oversized glob of mustard.

'Lovely dress Clare. Enjoying your evening?' I asked her. Cruel yes, but she had no idea I was crying of laughter on the inside.

'As a matter of fact, I am. Jason, *my* boyfriend, he's ex-military you know. Got his own business now', she gushed like a broken tap.

I resisted the urge to ask if it was in taxidermy.

'You should see him in his military dress coat, gorgeous.' She breathed at me and left, with no mention of her son's achievements.

To say we pissed ourselves of laughing, is an understatement. If anyone was going to fall for his bullshit, I was so glad that it was Clare. She deserved every happiness a man like that was going to bring her.

As we walked back to the auditorium, Cal was walking out towards me.

We all hugged him.

'Hey, you were amazing up there! Momma's got loads of photos, not saying she won't have chopped your head off on most of them, but part of you might be on them, maybe an ear.'

My mums' photography skills were legendary. Every birthday pic had a different body part on it, if you glued them all together, I'd be a whole person from different years.

'Oh god,' he smiled, 'You got a minute mum?'

I looked at him, 'Yeah course, you ok?'

'Yeah. Just wanted a word about something.'

The coven moved off and I led Cal to the foyer lounge where it was quiet. I hoped the pink dress hadn't broken his little heart.

He sighed, 'You're dating Mr Gilmore, aren't you?'

Oh shit. Shit. SHIT.

I wasn't about to lie to him; I just wish it had been another time.

I took a deep breath, 'Yes. I haven't said anything to you yet because, with the games coming up, I didn't want you distracted if you were going to be upset about it, and its early days and....'

He interrupted me, 'I knew before the game. Elliot told me. It's what's been upsetting him. His mum told him, and she said some really nasty things. He didn't know how or when to tell me.'

That poisonous bitch!

'Oh Cal. I'm so sorry you found out that way. Clare saw us out for lunch and, christ, I never thought she'd stoop so low. I didn't say anything because I didn't want *you* upset, but it seemed Clare didn't care about upsetting you *or* Elliot.'

I felt sick, it wasn't supposed to have come out like this.

'Elliot's had enough of living with his mum, he's going to go and live with his dad at the end of term. He says she's a nasty bitch.' He frowned.

Oh, she's a nasty bitch alright. What now? Had I ruined my son's big night?

Cal took a deep breath, 'Mum, I want you to know that I'm really happy for you. You've been different recently. You know, relaxed and happy and you haven't been like that for ages. If Andy, Mr Gilmore, makes you happy mum, don't let Elliot's mum ruin it. Mr Gilmore's awesome, he'll treat you properly and he's as mad as you are!' He smiled.

'Thank you. You've grown up into an amazing young man and so I'm proud of you.' I hugged him.

'Lexi isn't as chuffed though. Apparently, it's *urgh, gross*' he mimicked his sister, 'She'll get over it though. Zamir's about to ask her dance, so she'll be happy, she's been after him for ages.' And with that he wandered off to find his friends.

In the space of 5 minutes, I'd gone from concern, to dread, to anger, to bursting with pride and emotion. I needed a drink.

This called for vodka. I sat in the bar and tried to calm myself down, when Andy came in.

'Hey, I was just looking for you…'

I grabbed hold of him and kissed him, really kissed him, and I didn't care in that moment, who saw us.

'Jesus, don't kiss me like that in public, I'm gonna have to wait a minute before I can walk out of here,' he whispered.

'Sorry. I just needed to do that. You were brilliant up there and you look, wow!' I paused briefly, 'I've just spoken to Cal.'

'About?' he looked apprehensive.

I told him about the conversation with Cal.

He held my hand, 'At least there are no secrets now. We can just get on with, getting on. You ok?'

'Yeah, I'm good. Can you walk now without poking someone's eye out?'

'Ha, just don't kiss me like that again…. until later.'

Later couldn't come soon enough.

We got back to our table; people had started dancing. I watched my kids laughing on the dance floor, the older two flirting with their whole lives ahead of them.

I saw my mum and Roger dance to Taylor Swift's Shake it Off…. it's a sight that will haunt me for years to come. My friends got up to join in and rescue them, everyone laughing and loving their time together.

As I sat there and watched the people that I loved the most in my world, I turned and looked at Andy.

In that moment, I realised that something in me had changed. I'd started the whole dating thing because *I* was ready to. I'd spent so long wearing somebody else's label, that I'd lost myself along that road. Throughout my adult life, I'd tried so hard to dance to someone else's tune, instead of my own.

I didn't feel lost anymore and that wasn't down to anyone else. That was down to me. I understood that I didn't *need* to be in a relationship, I'd chosen to be in one.

This part of my journey had led me down an unexpected path, but I'd found me again, and I rather liked who I was.

Was this finally the Happily Ever After that I knew I deserved?

I hoped so.

Acknowledgements

Without my family and friends, nothing would shine as bright. Thank you all for the adventures, the love and the laughter.

Printed in Great Britain
by Amazon

46957617R00121